THE CHRISTMAS HOUSE

by
Florence Witkop

Published by Forget Me Not Romances, a division of Winged Publications

ISBN-13: 9781720210528

Dear Reader:

This is a book about finding love in a small town. My hero and heroine are normal, well-adjusted people. No 'big problems' to overcome, 'horrible childhoods' to deal with or 'angst' to get past. Just nice, every-day people who aren't looking for love but find it in spite of themselves during a Christmas spent in the middle of a still-primitive area of the north woods in a house so far from the highway that, in winter it can only be reached by snowmobile.

The following tells a bit about *The Christmas House.* When you finish reading *The Christmas House,* if you'll take the time to post a review on Amazon, I'll be forever grateful! Just go to Amazon, type in The Christmas House by Florence Witkop, and follow the prompts to post your review.

Now, here's what *The Christmas House* is about:

More than anything, Abby Carr wants to own the house in the forest where she spent many happy, childhood summers and she can have it if she follows the rules her grandmother laid out for owning it.

Having quit her job and moved to the north woods of Minnesota to live there and eventually own the house in the forest, she moves in -- and realizes her grandmother wasn't specific about the requirements. Exactly what does 'living the old way' mean? And how can she 'make a living and become a permanent resident' when she can't find a job? But she'll do her best. Until, on her very first day she gets between a mother bear and its cubs and barely escapes with her life. Things go downhill from there and only the help of her hunky neighbor promises to get her through the year alive and undamaged.

Bruce Merriweather grew up in the wilderness and pretty much knows everything there is to know about

living in the forest and is willing to tutor Abby if she'll pay for the lessons with her to-die-for muffins, which he dearly loves.
Muffins? Really!
With no other options, she reluctantly agrees, ignoring his effect on her libido because both of them are too busy surviving in the forest to have time for romance. But romance has a way of sneaking into any and all hearts and Christmas in the forest is the perfect time and place for love.

So now you know a bit about *The Christmas House*. If you'd like to learn more about my journey as a writer, about the books and short stories I've authored, or learn my thoughts on writing fiction, check out my website at http://www.FlorenceWitkop.com
Again, thanks for downloading *The Christmas House*.

Florence Witkop

PROLOGUE

"I agree that you were smart when you moved to the Caribbean." Maude Carr pushed her lemonade around the table, shading her eyes from the uber-bright sky while greedily absorbing the heat that fell around her and her friends like a living, breathing thing. "My old bones are in love with this place."

"I knew you'd like it." Charlene, her best friend since they'd pushed strollers together in Minnesota, squeezed between Maude and the third member of their party, Amity, who'd recently moved from Chicago to the Caribbean and was lonely for these friends who had nothing to hold them back from moving there, too, if she could talk them into it. Charlene had been easy, Maude not so much. Until now.

As Charlene plunked her ample bottom on a chair and made a noise that couldn't possibly be interpreted as any known word but clearly meant she was oh-do-comfortable, she asked, in a voice that said this wasn't the first time she'd asked this particular question, "Does that mean you've made up your mind? Finally? At long last?"

Maude sighed deeply. "I think so." She drained her lemonade in one long gulp and poured herself another. "Yes, I have. I'll move to the Caribbean, buy the condo between the two of yours and live a life of ease right here on this lovely beach."

Charlene cheered and waved her lemonade like a flag. "About time and you won't regret it for a second. No snow so high you can't walk through it, no cold wind, no thirty below zero mornings."

Amity also filled her glass from the frosty pitcher in the middle of the table. "What about your property? Don't you own land somewhere in northern Minnesota? I believe you said it included the shore along half a lake, a whole bunch of trees, and a cabin."

"It's not a cabin." Maude's answer was automatic because people who'd never visited her second home didn't realize that it was as solidly built as her contractor husband had been able to construct, never mind that the original had been a one-room settler's cabin. What was left of that cabin was now a few, old beams that Maude thought so beautiful that he'd salvaged them and used them to frame the huge stone fireplace in the main room, placing them as carefully as an artist might place a painting on a specific wall for best effect.

Though the house wasn't grand on the scale of many lakeshore mansions belonging to wealthy Minnesotans, it was what Maude had wanted and he'd built it for her, not for show. Sturdy, with super insulated walls that could take the worst weather that Minnesota could throw at it and laugh because she'd spent enough winters as a child shoving wood into the stove that had heated the entire original cabin to appreciate a truly weatherproof home. And easy to care for and live in, no matter that there were no electric lines anywhere nearby, the huge generator was more than adequate with a storage tank in the ground that held enough fuel for an entire year. Or two.

Maude scowled. "Good question. What to do with the forest house? That could be a problem." The house was exactly what she'd wanted, and the sturdy building reminded her of her late husband. She couldn't simply sell it to anyone with a checkbook. No, the new owner must love it as much as she did and must also love the lake it overlooked and the forest that surrounded it. "I admit that I don't know what to do with it but I can't bear to sell it to just anyone and I don't want it to fall apart from neglect once I move because I'll no longer be around to be sure it's cared for."

Charlene sipped her lemonade and nibbled a mango. "Don't you have several grandchildren? Can't you give it to one of them?" The three women were financially comfortable enough that giving away one house, no matter how large, wouldn't impoverish any of them.

Maude sighed. "Unfortunately, that would pose a problem. I have four grandchildren. Which one would I give it to and how would I do so without insulting the others?"

They all three went silent for a long time, thinking. Then Maude grinned. Her eyes lit up. She raised her glass in a grand gesture and the other ladies waited to hear what she'd decided to do with a huge tract of forest bordering a lake that was miles from the town of Johns Falls and had been in her family since forever but was reached only along a mile-long, primitive driveway that wasn't plowed in the winter and was marginal for getting to the highway safely no matter what season it was.

But Maude's smile didn't dim. Instead it grew. And grew. Because she had an idea. "I'll give it to whichever of my grandchildren will agree to quit their job and live in the house for a year -- in the old way as much as possible, I think, because that'll make the whole thing harder, make sure that whomever moves there wants it badly enough to work for it -- and in that year, whichever grandchild takes me up on my offer must figure out a way to make a living in the wilds of northern Minnesota. And stay there. Live there. Permanently."

"Impossible." Her friends looked at her as if she'd lost her mind. "No one will take you up on your offer. And why would they? It's a vacation place in a vacation area. It's not a permanent home."

But Maude kept smiling. "It can be a real home because it was my home when I was a child and I want it to be someone's home again." Her smile widened as she thought of her four grandchildren. One especially. "And I know my grandchildren so I know which one will take me up on my offer. Only one will agree to such difficult terms and her name is Abby."

She explained. She loved her grandchildren equally but only Abby had spent summers with Maude in that very house in the forest in much the way Maude had lived as a small child. They'd eschewed most of the amenities her husband had so thoughtfully provided when he rebuilt her home into a gathering place for their extended family.

Abby had loved living without electricity, cooking outside in a wood fire ring, finding berries in the forest. Had seen it as a great adventure. Had loved the place as much as Maude, and now Maude had no doubt that Abby would quit her job in the blink of an eye and move north while her three male cousins would shudder at the thought of giving up their prestigious jobs for the wilds of northern Minnesota.

In fact, she'd bet on it. Was going to bet on it as soon as she returned home to close out her affairs before moving to the Caribbean. "I'll make the offer to all of them together, knowing that only Abby will take me up on it. That way it won't look like I'm showing favoritism and Abby will get what I want her to have and she'll move north and live in the house on the lake in the forest that I so loved as a child." She thought a bit more, still smiling. "One year, and then I'll turn the deed over to her. Just one year is all it will take."

CHAPTER 1

Abby closed the door and, after a moment's thought, didn't bother to lock it because no self-respecting burglar would drive down that horrible driveway just to break into what until yesterday had been an unoccupied house when there were so many extravagant summer cottages scattered along the shores of other lakes that could be reached and broken into without destroying a vehicle's undercarriage in the process.

She slid the unnecessary key into a crevice in one of the white pines that surrounded the house, hitched up her jeans, took a better hold on the bucket that would soon be full of wild strawberries, and set off on a journey to explore her new home and figure out how to survive for a year. She'd get a job in town, that was an easy and necessary decision – money was required to buy food -- but to live in the old way? She didn't know exactly what that entailed but figured wild strawberries would be a start.

As she walked, she thought so hard that she scowled and almost tripped over the root of a tree that was on the almost non-existent path she and her grandmother had followed so many years earlier to reach the strawberry patch she sought now.

What exactly did Grandma Maude mean by that odd condition she'd placed on owning the piece of property that was an important part of her childhood? Was electricity allowed? Or not? There had been electricity in the Johns Falls area way back when, but not in this particular house when her grandmother was growing up and it only existed now because of the huge generator her grandfather had insisted on installing.

And what about becoming self-sufficient and a part of the community? Wasn't she already self-sufficient? An adult supporting herself, albeit at a low-wage job, but that would have changed eventually, she would have been promoted, if she hadn't quit to move to the north woods. Besides, what did self-sufficiency in the north woods involve? And why hadn't her grandmother made it clear?

She thought further. If she turned off the generator because Grandma Maude hadn't had electricity growing up and that might be what 'the old way' involved, then she couldn't use the huge freezer in the basement that even now was stocked with enough food for an army for a year. Or for one five-foot two female for even longer. Because if she turned it off, then all that food would spoil. So, yes, the generator must be acceptable because Grandma Maude was thrifty and would never abide spoilage.

But could she use other electricity without breaking the terms of the agreement? If not everything, how much was allowed? Lights? Hot water? Cooking on the huge electric range that could feed an army or one hungry extended family? There was no TV, never had been, and she wouldn't miss it – much – but hot water would be nice, though not essential as she could heat water on the stove, if using the stove was allowed. And the dishwasher would be absolute luxury. She really wanted to use the dishwasher.

No dishwasher, she decided, telling herself sternly that it was a luxury, not a necessity, but maybe she could have hot water once in a while? She wished she knew. And electric lights in the evenings would be nice because there were no kerosene lamps in the house like the ones she and her grandmother had used. So maybe lights?

She sighed because the agreement was turning out to be more complicated than she'd thought when she'd jumped up and down at the idea of living in the forest house while her cousins had backed off so fast you'd think they were avoiding a poisonous snake. But how much electricity to use was a hard thing to figure.

She thought further. Part of the deal was that she had to make a living so maybe lights would be acceptable if she ended up needing them to get ready for work in the morning. Or find her purse. She decided she'd wing it as far as electricity was concerned. Hopefully she'd have an electric epiphany before arriving at the berry patch.

Heat was another concern. It was spring and warm but winter would come and she'd better know how Grandma wanted the house heated. The generator easily provided the minimal heat that kept the super-insulated, extremely efficient building warm, but there was also the huge stone fireplace that was absolutely beautiful and covered most of one wall and did a semi-adequate job of keeping the main rooms warm and was probably more along the lines of 'the old way.' The bedrooms would be cold but there wasn't much help for that. Except that they each had a bathroom and water pipes could freeze if the rooms weren't heated adequately and p lumbers were expensive. So, she had to keep the house warm or face dire consequences. But how to accomplish warmth?

The possibility that she could cut and haul and split enough wood herself to heat the house with the fireplace without killing herself was problematic at best and suicide at worst. And then she'd have to drag the pieces to the fireplace in the dead of winter through snow piled feet deep and then place them in it in such a way as to provide heat without causing a chimney fire, which was something she'd been warned about but didn't know how to avoid.

She paused as she passed the small pile of firewood on her way to the big woods, considered it gravely, knew it wasn't close to adequate, and decided she'd have to think further about heat. The fireplace versus electric heat. The old way that would guarantee eventual ownership of the forest house versus staying alive and warm.

So thinking, she was soon deep in the forest, not concerned about getting lost because her grandmother had made her walk the boundaries over and over until she knew exactly where they were and had then made her learn the entire property, all hundreds of acres of it, so she'd never need to be rescued. She knew every tree and boulder, every hill and marsh.

Of course, she thought ruefully as she cast a look around, that had been a long time ago. Years ago, and the forest changed constantly. She knew in a general way where she was, knew approximately where the patch of wild strawberries she sought grew, wasn't concerned about getting truly lost, as in needing to be rescued, but wasn't exactly sure where to find the tiny, sweet berries.

Then she saw them. "Hah! You're mine now." She speeded up, crashing through the brush. Until she heard a sound.

A growl, low and menacing.

She froze. Looked towards the sound. And realized, with a sinking heart and a feeling of sheer terror that a very large black bear stood mere yards away, looking at both her and something beyond her. She turned her head cautiously and saw the bear's twin cubs an equal distance away on her other side.

She was between a mother bear and its cubs. She was in serious danger. She could be mauled. Killed. She thought furiously, not moving a muscle, watching the mother bear but not knowing what to do. How to exit without it charging her. How to convince the bear that she, Abby, meant no harm. How to stay alive.

Something came beside her. Two somethings. She looked down without moving a muscle, just her eyes, and saw two very large dogs, one on either side, staring at the mother bear, teeth bared and growling themselves, daring it to attack, and then she saw a third dog, equally large, a few feet back. All threatening the bear as the bear threatened her. They were protecting her. Not backing an inch. As aggressive as the bear itself.

She gave thanks for the dogs. Prayed. Hoped that their presence meant she might live.

"Don't move." The whisper near her ear was the most welcome sound she'd ever heard. After the dogs' growls, of course. "The bear will take movement for aggression. But don't let it know that you're afraid, either, or it'll attack because it'll believe you won't fight back."

"What should I do?" Her whisper, without moving her lips, was hoarse with fear and soft enough that the bear didn't pay her any closer attention than before. Just kept growling. And shaking its head as bears do when they are threatening something. Or someone.

Large, muscular arms wrapped slowly around her from behind and pulled her just as slowly against an equally muscular chest, then pressed her so firmly to a rather large body that she couldn't move if she tried. "When I say 'three,' we'll both very, very slowly back away until she no longer sees you as a threat to her cubs. Just come with me, one step at a time, and I promise that we'll get out of this alive. The dogs will keep her occupied enough that she won't charge while we're getting the heck out of here."

The dogs snarled louder, the bear growled again, a throaty, menacing sound that sent chills down Abby's spine, as it again moved its huge head from side to side, thinking what to do, how to get to its cubs. How to eliminate the threat to her babies.

"Remember, when I say 'three.' As we back, wave your arms. Yell. Look bigger than you are and be loud. Let her think that together we are a huge, dangerous monster that she'd better not tangle with."

Grandma Maude had said much the same thing long, long ago when they were walking in the forest. How to behave if a bear appeared. But she'd never said what to do if they were between a bear and its cubs.

"One. Two. Threeeeee." Held so tight to her savior's chest that she couldn't have moved on her own if she'd tried, Abby felt herself being slowly hauled backwards. She raised her arms and waved them about. Yelled though not loud enough to scare anything because she was so scared that she could hardly manage a whisper.

Miraculously, the bear stopped growling. Paused. Looked. Stopped shaking its head. Was uncertain, off guard "Yell louder. Scream for your life. Give the dogs some help."

She wasn't sure she could make a loud sound over her terror but she tried. And she did it. She suddenly had the ability to scream like a banshee and so did the man holding her so tight that they might as well be one person, moving them both backwards one tiny step at a time. adding his very loud baritone to her shrill, terrified soprano as her arms wind-milled through the air.

Step by step they backed away from the bear until they were no longer between the mother and its cubs, at which moment the mother bear made a different sound and the cubs moved, scampering through the underbrush until they were with their mother once more.

With which the mother and cubs turned and disappeared, though the three dogs remained where they were, on guard, still snarling, and with teeth bared until the man holding Abby tight to his body whistled. Then they moved, wagging their tails and jumping on Abby and her savior as if they were a puppy threesome.

Abby sagged against whoever was holding her,

hoping he'd not let go any time soon because if he did, she'd fall. She was that scared. But he kept a grip even as he carefully turned her around so they were face to face and she found herself looking up into a very male face, all angles and planes and dark hair and eyes, with eyebrows that were pushed up in question. "And how did you happen to get between a mother bear and its cubs anyway?

She opened her mouth to speak. Found she couldn't. Tried again. Managed to croak out a few words. "I was looking for strawberries."

He nodded, still holding her, though now away from his body as he tested her ability to stand on her own, even as the dogs tried to climb up his body seeking affection and acknowledgement that they'd done well. He cautiously let go of her enough to use one hand to shower them with love and, realizing that the dogs had most likely saved her life, Abby did the same, pushing away the hand that still held her so she could drop to her knees and hug all three dogs at once. Because they were wonderful. Amazing. Because she loved them even though less than a minute earlier she'd not known them at all.

"You were looking for strawberries." He thought over her words. "So was the momma bear, only she was here first."

"I didn't see her." Abby took a deep breath and remembered all those lessons about the wilderness all those years ago. "I should have been watching, I know. I forgot." Don't forget anything, ever, her grandmother had said, because the wilderness doesn't forgive mistakes easily.

"That's what I figured when I saw you head right

for the berries without looking either right or left."

"How come --? What are you --? Why are you here --?"

He shrugged simply. "Same as you and the bears. Strawberries." He pointed to a small, empty bucket nearby. "Unlike you, however, I noticed the bear and was waiting until she and her cubs had had enough. Then I planned to pick what was left."

Abby rocked back on her heels, still hugging the three dogs in a huge embrace. "What are their names?" So she could thank them individually.

"Paris, London and Madrid." The names were so unexpected that Abby found herself laughing. Moments earlier she'd have said she'd never laugh again but now she giggled, then chuckled, then laughed out loud and her savior grinned along with her as he explained. "Places I never expect to visit but they must be nice places so I figured I'd honor them this way." He tousled the dogs' heads. "Madrid is the youngest but he's no slouch. If Paris and London hadn't been on either side of us, then he'd have been there with bells on."

Abby suddenly remembered that this was her grandmother's property and that this man, whoever he was, however glad she was that he was there saving her life, was trespassing. Not that she cared and as far as she was concerned he could trespass any time he wanted. Forever and beyond. But she was curious. "Are you from around here?" Locals traipsed about the woods as they pleased, knowing exactly whose property they were on while knowing that the owner wouldn't mind. Was that the case with her savior?

He pointed with his chin. "I own the property on the other side of the lake -- a few acres -- and I share the driveway with the owner of this particular piece of property. We met last year and she gave me permission to wander about. So that's my story." He gave her a curious look. "But who are you and why are you trespassing in Maude's woods?"

Really? He owned the property on the other side of the lake that used to belong to an elderly man she and her grandmother visited now and then. Until his house burned down and he moved to town. And this was the new owner and he shared a driveway with her. She nodded shortly because it all made sense and she'd just met her neighbor. "I'm Abby. I'm Maude's granddaughter and so I share the driveway with you and I'm going to own this property in a year."

Then honesty compelled her to add, "I hope."

CHAPTER 2

Hiding his surprise, the stranger held out a hand. "Hello, Abby, nice to meet you." He thought back on the last few moments. "I'm Bruce and I'm glad neither of us got eaten today."

He tipped his head to think and Abby saw his eyes turn momentarily even darker than before. What color were they? She didn't have a clue, just that they were dark as a starlit night. "I have a suggestion, Abby." She waited, unable to guess what he was about to say but not expecting what he said. "Since we share a driveway and its maintenance, what say we get together one of these days to discuss the care and feeding of that horrible stretch of gravel that is determined to destroy any vehicle that uses it even once?"

Abbey was still shaking from residual fear and laughing because the dogs were wonderful and then, with his comment, wanted to giggle also. Most of all, though she didn't wish to be alone in a part of the forest that held a mother bear and its cubs and it was a long walk back to the house. The bears could be met again on that walk. "How about now at my place?"

He pursed his lips and his eyes went darker, she'd bet on it, becoming the night sky without stars, and she shivered because she'd never seen that in anyone before. Or because she was still terrified and when people were afraid they shook. He spoke carefully, knowing exactly how she felt, knowing she didn't want to be alone in the forest, reading her fear. "You mean after we get our fill of strawberries?" Reminding her why they'd all come to this place and, yes, she'd forgotten.

"Of course. That's what I meant." Strawberries were why she'd come and were what had gotten her into this mess. "After we fill our buckets."

He examined the strawberry patch. "I doubt there are that many berries but we can get what's here." His face kind of fell because he'd clearly wanted a lot of strawberries and would have to do with a few. "Then we can go someplace and talk."

"And eat strawberries." She hoped the bear family had left more strawberries than what she could see in a quick look but wasn't sure. "Unless you plan to freeze your share instead of eating them."

He laughed, a pleasant, self-deprecating sound. "You're kidding, right? I only turn on my generator a couple hours a day. Not enough to keep a freezer operational."

Of course he had a generator. There was no power to either property along the driveway and as for where he lived, there hadn't been a house on the adjoining property since fire took the original cabin and there were no signs of the kind of traffic on the driveway that building one would necessitate.

So where did he live? In what? She couldn't guess but tucked his comment about a generator two hours a day as maybe being a way of having the best of two worlds. The old and the new. Maybe she could do the same and her grandmother would be happy. If two hours would keep the freezer cold. "So, you plan to eat your berries immediately?"

He shrugged. "If there are left-overs, I'll make jam." Shrugged again. "No electricity needed."

"You make jam?"

"Of course. Don't you?"

She didn't but it seemed like a good skill to acquire if she was to live the old way. She shook her head, looked at her bucket, and headed for the now safe strawberry patch to see how full she could get it. He picked up his own and joined her and soon they were moving small, red berries from plants to pails, crawling on their hands and knees while shoving aside dogs who wanted to play now that their work was done and their master was safe and who thought they were on the ground for fun.

When there weren't any ripe berries left, they rose. Abby stretched the kinks from her back, pointed the way, and set off for her grandmother's house, followed by Bruce what's-his-name. No, that wasn't right. Not her grandmother's house. Hers. Maybe. Hopefully. No matter how many momma bears got between her and her goal. No matter how many mistakes she made while learning to live in the wilderness. She'd become the owner of a piece of northern Minnesota forest that she'd loved since she was a child or she'd die trying though she sincerely hoped that last wouldn't happen.

When they reached her grandmother's house – *her* house someday – she felt rather than heard Bruce what's-his-name draw a deep breath. She turned and found him staring at the elegant, Victorian building with a three-car attached garage and shaking his head in what seemed like awe.

She tried to look at the house through his eyes. It wasn't near the size of the suburban house she grew up in. But he seemed to see it differently and she wondered why as she led the way across the deck that overlooked the lake and into the great room with its sliding glass doors and high ceilings and the huge fireplace because that was what her grandfather had built.

As Bruce stepped inside, he turned his head to take in the large, central room and the smaller rooms off of it, the master bedroom and bath and the second room with its own bathroom that had served various purposes over the years. Then up the stairs and he could only guess how many rooms were up there.

She read his question. "Four. There are four bedrooms upstairs and four more bathrooms."

He flushed and looked abruptly away, striding towards the kitchen island and setting his bucket down. "Sorry. I didn't mean to stare."

She smiled. "It's okay to stare at this particular house because my grandfather designed and built it himself." She decided to be completely honest. "With the help of his entire crew because he was a contractor."

"And now it's yours." That touch of awe returned to his voice though he tried to disguise it.

She decided to be honest once more. "It will be

mine. In a year. If I fulfill the conditions my grandmother set."

He looked around again. "Whatever those conditions are, I'd jump through a million hoops if I could own this place." He looked through the plate glass windows to the lake that shimmered in the sun. "I'd do whatever it took."

She dropped to one of the stools at the kitchen island. "I hope I can. I'm not sure, though."

His eyebrows creased and she explained the conditions that lay between her and possession of the house in the forest. He pursed his lips. "So you plan on heating this place with a fireplace?" She nodded and his eyes rolled in disbelief. "The entire house?" rolled his eyes again. "Do you know how much wood that would take, not to mention that it's impossible because there are no heat ducts from the fireplace?"

"If it's a condition of owning this place, then I'll do it. I'll do whatever I have to do." She stuck out her lower lip. "Like you would if you were in my place."

He studied her a moment. "Do you have a chain saw to cut trees with?"

"There's one in the basement."

"Do you know how to use it?"

"I can figure it out."

He put his hands on either side of his head and shook it slowly from side to side. "You'll die. Or else you'll become a bloody mess and I'll have to bring you to the hospital because no ambulance could possibly get down that driveway." Shook his head again. "Let me tell you something and please listen. You can't heat this large a building with that fireplace. Can't."

"I'm afraid that electric heat might not be

acceptable and, if it isn't, I won't get the place."

"You have electric heat? You can be warm by simply flipping a switch?"

"Yes but that's not the old way."

He groaned. "Lord help me, the mother bear and her cubs were just the beginning. I'm going to have to hold your hand for a year to keep you alive and in reasonably good health."

She stood up, stung. "You don't have to do anything. Nothing at all. It's my life, my choice and it'll be my house in a year."

"If you live the old way, which you don't seem to know how to do."

"I can learn. There are books."

He came beside her. "Hey, I didn't mean to anger you. But the old way can be dangerous. I know." He took a deep breath, looked over the lake again, then around the large room that was the center of the house that would someday be hers. "Because it so happens that I'm an expert at exactly what you need to know."

"How to live the old way?"

He made a wry face. "My parents were hippies. *Are* hippies. They went back to nature before it was fashionable. So, yes, I know how to live the old way and I see that I must do a lot of teaching in the next few months because I don't want to have to drag you to the hospital. Or worry that you'll be doing something stupid when I'm not around. Like cutting down trees and splitting wood when you don't know how to do either."

He stared at her, up and down and sidewise, and took a huge breath. "I'm going to do it whether you want me to or not. As a favor to Maude because she's a very nice lady. I wouldn't feel at all good if I let her granddaughter cut off an arm or leg or freeze to death or in any other way come to misfortune while I'm around to prevent it."

Abby didn't know what to say because his offer was so absolutely what she wanted – needed – but the way it had been put made her feel like an idiot. Which she probably was if she thought she could do this, could live in the house in the forest in the old way for an entire year. "It gets worse. I also have to find a way to make a living so I can stay here permanently. I must become a part of the community and become self-sufficient."

He dropped to the counter and pounded it a few times. "Really? Self-sufficient? You?" He looked her up and down again, all five feet two inches of citified female. "And how do you propose to support yourself in the middle of the forest?"

She licked her lips. "There are ways. I'll get a job." She gave him a cunning look. "You make a living – somehow." She looked at him expectantly. "How do you make a living?"

He wagged his head from side to side slowly before answering. "I was a medic in Afghanistan. When I came home I took a course in medical billing and I now do that from my home. It's why I have a generator, for power to get my work done and get hot water once a day. Otherwise I wouldn't bother with electric at all." He blinked. "So what did you do before you moved to the wilderness?"

In a very small voice, she said, "I sold dresses in a boutique." His groan said what he thought of the possibility of making a living selling upscale dresses in the north woods. "I'll think of something. Go to town. Find a job."

"And not be able to get to your job in the winter." Then he sighed for about the hundredth time. "Unless I get you there on my snowmobile. You can leave your car at the end of the driveway, it's where I keep mine when the snow comes. Snowmobile along the driveway then drive the truck to town."

She drew into herself, he saw it happen and she watched him watch her. It was an odd sensation. Then she sat up straighter and he knew – and she knew that he knew -- that there was something of her grandmother in her after all, some of the spunk he must have seen in the elderly lady, some of the fire. "I'll figure something." She brushed imaginary crumbs from her pants.

He went silent, they both did, until he turned to the strawberries and changed the topic. "What say we clean and eat them? A half a bowl each and we don't have to make jam because there aren't enough. Not many at all, not after those bears had their fill."

She was more than happy to change the subject. She examined their booty. "I think there are enough for muffins if you can stick around long enough for me to bake them."

"Muffins?" His attention was pricked.

"My grandmother and I used to make them with all sorts of berries that we picked in the woods. And she had a berry patch in a sunny spot beside the house."

"A berry patch? Is it still there?" Abby said she didn't know, hadn't checked, had only arrived the day before. He pulled her from her stool. "Let's see."

Five minutes later, they added a generous bucket of

additional strawberries to what they'd picked in the forest. "Enough for a feast and some left over." He started rinsing them in the sink before she could tell him not to use the running water. "I love muffins. If you want to make a million muffins I'll fight a million bears if I can have some."

And suddenly, they weren't discussing the very depressing subject of her survival for an entire year. Instead they were working side by side in the kitchen as she and her grandmother had done all those years earlier. Cleaning berries, finding the recipe tucked somewhere in a cupboard, she didn't know where at first but finally found it, almost unreadable because of flour and butter smeared across it.

Soon they were measuring and mixing and adding berries and baking and as the sun shone through the huge windows her grandfather had insisted on, she knew she was in the right place, doing the right thing, and that this house and all those berries, both in the forest and in the berry patch beside the house would be hers someday. As soon as she figured out what 'the old way' consisted of and how to avoid disaster for a year and how to get a job.

When the muffins were done and slathered with butter even before being cool, and they'd each sampled a couple – or three-- all Bruce what's-his-name said was, "If you keep me supplied with these heavenly muffins then I'll do my best – or at least what's reasonable – to keep you alive and I'll do whatever else is necessary to make sure that you'll be here for the rest of my life so I can continue to enjoy the best muffins on earth and enjoy them forever."

His speech was followed by a contented sigh, after

which he gathered three very large dogs and left, leaving Abby wondering what his last name was until she decided that all that mattered was that his first name was Bruce and he lived next door -- as next door was measured in the forest -- and that he'd help her get through the coming year and he'd do it because her grandmother's recipe made the best muffins on earth.

And because, she decided as she opened a can of cold spaghetti for dinner, he was nice as well as one of the best-looking guys she'd seen in a long time. All those muscles. Living in the forest was a great workout.

CHAPTER 3

The next day, Abby didn't turn on the lights, which was easy because daylight came early and lasted late in the north woods in the summer. And examined the huge fireplace closely and decided that if she could get enough split wood to keep it going for the entire winter without actually having to split the wood herself – maybe she could buy some? -- she'd do so but if the wood pile died before spring and she had no idea how large a pile she'd need, well if that happened then she'd wimp out and heat the house with power from the generator.

Strike one against owning the house? Would her grandmother disapprove if she used electric heat? She didn't know, wondered if she dare ask when they spoke next or would just asking make her grandmother think she didn't deserve the house?

Hot water was different, she could heat that on the

stove if using the water heater was out of bounds. Which she didn't know. Another question to ask if she grew brave enough to question her grandmother. And what about the kitchen stove, anyway? Did using the six-burner electric range qualify as 'the old way?' Probably not. She went outside to check out the outdoor stove her grandfather had built, brick by brick, complete with an oven large enough to hold a full-sized pig or a few dozen hamburgers.

It was so huge that filling it with the wood that fired it and then getting it going would be a major chore but she decided that she could possibly do so once a week and cook an entire week's worth of meals at one time. But she'd have to use the kitchen oven for all those muffins that were what would get her through the year alive if her next-door neighbor meant what he said about helping her if he could be paid in muffins.

The whole thing was way too complicated. But she'd quit her job immediately after the meeting with her grandmother and started packing as soon as the job was history. Now she wondered if, when her cousins backed away from Grandma Maude's proposal in absolute horror, they'd had the right idea after all.

No they didn't. She wanted this property – loved this place – and would do whatever it took. She'd start by carrying water from the lake to clean the house. It wasn't exactly dirty but had been unoccupied for quite a while so there was a thin layer of dust everywhere. But there were buckets and mops and everything else necessary to make it shine and she was young and strong and would have the place gleaming in no time. She would. Absolutely.

Many hours later, she sagged onto a deck chair and

wondered what she'd gotten herself in for while wondering how pioneer women had managed to have clean houses. Or maybe they didn't, compared to today's homes, because cleaning the old way was hard work.

As she scowled at the lake that glittered like a million diamonds in the breeze that ruffled the surface, she heard a movement in the nearby woods. She froze. Got ready to run inside and get a baseball bat in case the mother bear had learned where she lived and was about to punish her for scaring her babies in the strawberry patch.

But no bears appeared. Instead, three dogs and Bruce what's-his-name strolled across the small clearing in which the house sat and stepped onto the deck, after which Bruce dropped into the chair next to hers. "Hi."

"Hi." She waited. Why was he there?

"I'm here for muffins if you have more. And to discuss the driveway, which we forgot about the other day."

"No muffins yet." She scowled again at the brightly lit, sunshiny, happy lake. How dare it look so cheerful when she was so exhausted? "I've been cleaning house."

He examined her minutely, then rolled his eyes and shook his head. "Judging from your expression you've been doing it the same way my mom did before she and my dad decided that with experience came wisdom and had electricity run to the farm. Electricity is wonderful, you know. All that amazing power that magically appears at the flick of a switch and that you could be using right now if you weren't so set on doing everything the hard way."

"The old way, not the hard way. Because that might be what my grandmother meant for me to do."

He stared at her as if to make sure she was sane. "Our ancestors weren't stupid. They did whatever was easiest and they did it with whatever was handy and I see a lot of switches on walls if you'd just flick them once in a while."

"I can carry water." Another roll of his eyes that she ignored. "And heat it on the outdoor stove."

He leaned a bit to see the brick monster beside the deck that she knew could be fired up and that had cooked many meals when the family had gathered when she was young but that wasn't worth the effort to heat a bucket of water. He snorted. "You are using cold lake water because you don't want to fire up that behemoth."

"It isn't exactly cold. I could swim in it if I chose."

Another derisive snort. "But you don't because you don't have the time. And when you finish cleaning you're too tired."

"I might go for a swim."

This time he didn't snort, just closed his eyes and shook his head. Again. "You won't use that perfectly beautiful shower in the house because you're scared you won't inherit this house." He looked around and sighed and she could sense him turning that thought over in his mind. Because the house was worth a lot of effort.

She slid lower into her chair, hunching her shoulders against his silent laughter. "Nothing wrong with bathing in the lake. It's clean."

He came to a conclusion about how much work was enough and how much was too much. Then he came to stand over her, one hand on either side of her chair. Touched her shoulders accidentally and sent electricity through her body. A residual effect of the bear encounter. Must be. Couldn't be anything else, which meant it would subside over time. "You are not thinking clearly." He took a deep breath. "No grandmother in the world would require such sacrifice on the part of a beloved grandchild." Another breath, minty, like the forest. "Besides, if you get a job in town, which you pretty much must do if you're going to stay here forever, you'll need to be clean and I doubt you'll break the ice to bathe in the lake in the middle of winter."

She slid deeper into her chair and refused to look at him. "I'll figure that out later." She changed the subject. "I thought you were the bear coming through the forest."

He stood straight, a tall, blocky shadow against the sun. "Actually, that's why I'm here." As her eyes adjusted to the light, she saw him clearly again. Those amazing dark eyes, dark hair, skin brown from being outside, muscles taut, a body honed by hard work. And full of the electricity she'd just felt. "I've seen the momma bear a few times since our encounter in the strawberry patch." He frowned and this time not because he was criticizing her choice of lifestyle, rather from easily read and very real concern. "Each time it happened, I'd not have known she was nearby if not for the dogs. They alerted me and we got out of her way as fast as possible."

"I don't have a dog." She frowned uneasily. "So maybe I'll stay out of the woods." She didn't want to be limited to the small clearing around the house but what else could she do? "Do you think she'll come here? To the house? "

He nodded, eyes flicking around the small cleared area. "Of course she will, especially if you cook outside and that's another reason not to use this outdoor grill. The smell of food will bring her as surely as my name is Bruce Merriweather. And you'll not know she's here until she's inches away and what will you do then?"

Abby shrank into herself and spoke in a very small voice. "I don't know."

He nodded as if that was the first sensible thing she'd said since he arrived. "And you have a berry patch and she likes berries and that's why I'm here."

"For berries?"

"To protect you from bears. From one bear in particular. I have three dogs and you have none though all you need is one dog to alert you if she comes around. So I'm leaving one dog here." She drew in her breath because that wasn't what she'd expected but it made such sense that she felt a small trickle of warmth and gratitude. "Any of the three though I strongly suggest London or Paris because experience matters in bear encounters and they have lots so either of them will keep her and her cubs at bay long enough for you to get inside."

Abby licked her lips. She'd not expected to have to deal with wildlife, had never had to when a small child wandering the property with her grandmother. Of course, her grandmother had grown up tramping those very acres and knew both the forest and the animals that lived there intimately. And, now that she thought about it, her grandmother's huge dog had always been with them. Every single time.

"I thank you and I'll be grateful for whichever one wants to stay."

It was decided that London would move in with Abby because he didn't shed quite as much as the other two and she found two rather large bowls to hold the dog food Bruce Merriweather had brought – she knew his last name now – and enough water to keep London happy.

It was lake water because she wasn't using the kitchen sink. "Pioneers didn't have faucets that brought forth water at the flick of a wrist." Before he could laugh or say a word, she tipped her nose up a bit and filled a bucket from the lake and set it next to London's water bowl so she could fill it easily though he'd probably ignore the bowl and go straight for the bucket.

But Bruce now-she-knew-his-name wasn't done. "Those pioneers did have wells and pumps that worked almost as well as faucets so I don't see why you're torturing yourself by carrying buckets from the lake just to prove a point."

He meandered into the kitchen, found a glass from a cupboard and poured himself a glass of water from the faucet. Just because he could and, probably, to prove a point. "So think over that little fact and think hard about whether you want to carry water from the lake when there's a couple feet of snow to be tramped through or whether you want to do what your ancestors did and get water from the kitchen, even if you use a faucet and they used a hand pump." He put down the empty glass and wiped his mouth. "And now if it's at all possible I'd love some more of your grandmother's muffins and I believe that the only way to get some is to turn on that beautiful electric range that's standing idle against the wall doing absolutely nothing and help you bake pretty much as we did the other day."

He looked about the kitchen. The closed cupboards and the counters with nothing on them. "Right after we adjourn to that beautiful garden that's full of berries that I believe you forgot exists because you've been so busy carrying water from the lake and cleaning a house that's already clean except for a few specks of dust here and there."

He took a deep breath and continued. "We will go to that garden and pick some strawberries and plop them down on these lovely counters and then we will get to work." He examined her gravely. "Unless you wish to let those strawberries rot on the vine while you continue to do more work than our ancestors dreamed of."

Abby swallowed any reply she might have been thinking and didn't argue because she was exhausted and strawberry muffins did sound wonderful. She grabbed a bucket and followed him outside and ate as many strawberries as she put in her bucket because, yes, she had forgotten about the garden and, yes, they were wonderful and, yes, she had been too busy washing away dust to think beyond opening a can of whatever was in the cupboard for dinner and eating the contents cold but she chose not to mention that fact because it probably wasn't what pioneers did. Or what Bruce Merriweather did.

Several hours later they sat on the deck and ate muffins along with the lovely meal she'd prepared on the stove because as long as she was using the oven she might as well use the burners also. She decided she'd forgotten how delicious hot food could be and soon wished she'd not eaten so much because her stomach was uncomfortably full and she didn't care, she simply ate another muffin and decided that she'd be eternally grateful to her grandmother for not taking the recipe with her when she moved to the Caribbean.

And somehow time passed and they were still sitting on the deck when the moon rose and its bright light tipped the surface of the lake with almost the same silver as the sun had done earlier and the dogs napped beside and around them and a stiff wind ruffled the surface of the lake and kept the daytime diamonds glittering and the mosquitoes at bay and Abby wished that time would stop and had the oddest feeling that Bruce was thinking the same thing and she had no idea where that thought came from because she normally couldn't read other peoples' thoughts but she could this one time.

Eventually, Bruce rose and called the two dogs that would accompany him home and make sure there was no bear nearby to disturb his walk. And hovered over Abby as if about to say something. Tall and solid and protective in a way she'd never thought she'd need or even want but was glad to have living near enough to help if help was needed. And touched her lightly. Just touched her and that electricity went through her again, only it hadn't diminished as she'd expected. Instead it had ramped up a notch and she wondered what would happen in the future. Would she turn into a shower of sparks when he touched her again?

And then, as thoughts swirled through her mind, he left, silently, disappearing into the forest with London watching, ears lifted towards his master's passage even as he also watched over Abby and she was as glad for his alertness as she was for the fact that a very knowledgeable pioneer type lived nearby.

This living in the wilderness thing wasn't what she'd expected, what she'd thought it would be. Not at all. But it was still what she wanted, perhaps even more than when her grandmother first proposed it, and she didn't know why that was, what about it appealed to her so much. But it did and she determined to gather her courage and ask her grandmother for particulars regarding the conditions of owning the land when they next spoke.

CHAPTER 4

A couple days later, Saturday morning, she headed for town because she'd brought minimal supplies and needed a few things. Soap, shampoo, more canned goods and mosquito repellant. She was also determined to find the job that would enable her to live here permanently and the sooner she started her search the better. Maybe not actually fill out applications but get a feel for the way things were in Johns Falls. See what was out there. And enjoy a meal she hadn't cooked, preferably the kind found in fast food places that sent health nuts into overdrive. A burger and fries or a huge slice of gooey pizza.

She drove slowly and carefully along the driveway so as to save the undercarriage on her tiny Chevy that was great for city driving but wasn't built for the kind of torture it would be subjected to every time she left her forest home. Since she couldn't afford another car she'd best take care of the one she had. Yes, her parents had offered to help her buy a sturdier car when she moved north, but she'd nixed their help because she wanted to do this on her own.

Eventually, she reached the highway and then the town of Johns Falls, already filling with a few tourists and people who owned summer places on the many lakes scattered throughout the area. There was an air of laid-back charm in the slow way people sauntered along the sidewalks and meandered over the grass-covered park and examined the goods for sale in the tourist-oriented stores between the grain elevator at one end of town and the church at the other. Sunglasses were in abundance and she decided to get a pair, along with a huge sun hat similar to those a few women wore.

But first she'd check for 'help wanted' signs. Which she soon learned were non-existent. She should have known there'd be none because summer help had long ago been hired so as to be trained in before the first wave of tourists arrived. She wilted with concern and, seeing that it was close to lunch time, turned into Jerry's Pizza that also, if she remembered correctly, served the best cappuccinos in northern Minnesota. Maybe, if he wasn't busy, Jerry would know someone who needed help.

He didn't. He did remember her once she told him who she was. "You've grown a whole lot," was his dry comment as he backed a bit to examine her better. "In a good way." Then, "Is your grandma with you?"

She explained that her grandmother was in the Caribbean and that, if things went right, she, Abby, would become a permanent Johns Falls resident. "Glad to have you in the neighborhood. Nice lady, your grandmother. None better. Her family's been around for generations so I can see why she'd want someone in the family to come back and live in the old place."

He shuddered. "Awful driveway, though. Better plan on a new one or at least a four-wheel drive vehicle." He thought a moment. "And a snowmobile in the winter. I think that guy who bought the neighboring property – what's his name? – Bruce something – that's what he uses." He nodded. "Yep, if you don't want to be stuck there all winter, you should consider one or the other."

She explained that she'd need a job if she was to do anything at all, but he just pursed his lips and shook his head. "Wrong time of year to find a job." But he promised to keep an eye out for any opportunities and he took her cell number and said he'd call if he heard of anything. Then he served her the wonderful pizza that she remembered from her childhood along with a cappuccino that would make any New York barista proud and then turned away to serve other customers who'd been waiting patiently for their turns.

Later, wearing both sunglasses that hid her disappointment at not finding a variety of available jobs, and a hat that was the epitome of tourist chic, she took a foot tour of the tiny town before shopping for supplies and returning home. She noticed signs with huge arrows that proclaimed a farmers' market and craft fair in the newish park on the river's edge where visitors could watch the falls that gave Johns Falls its name while shopping for totally unnecessary but nice things to bring home along with some very wonderful produce.

She didn't need anything for the house, thank you very much, it was well furnished, but maybe some produce would be nice and she'd never been to the park because it had been created since her last visit. So she followed the signs and soon found herself walking along a series of blindingly white canopies under which all sorts of fascinating things were for sale.

One of the canopies held a collection of rather nice pictures painted on birch bark, all very lovely but she had no space on her walls. She was about to continue to the next display when a voice stopped her. "Hey. Abby."

She found herself looking into the eyes of her neighbor, the very dark eyes and hair and face of planes and angles topping the muscular body that had walked her back from a potentially deadly bear encounter. The body that sent electric shocks through her whenever it touched hers.

The unexpectedness of seeing him in this place sent her back to that day, brought back the feel of his body, the whispered voice, the strength of his arms cocooning her, protecting her. As if it had just happened.

She shook the feeling away. "Hi. Bruce." Considered her neighbor behind a counter under a white canopy at a craft show. "What are you doing here?"

"Selling stuff." He waved to someone he knew, gave a couple potential customers who were pausing to examine his work a rundown on the picture they were considering, but when they left, he continued where he'd left off as if there'd been no pause. "I like making this stuff. I have a fun but totally useless minor in art and it brings in a bit of extra money, not to mention that it's a great way to meet people." With which he waved to a passing family, obviously tourists he knew well.

"From previous years. They like my stuff and have a lot of it on their walls."

"But you do medical billing for a living."

"Before my parents dropped out of normal society, my mother taught art at the University. You should see their house now. It's gorgeous and, since she didn't know how to stop teaching art, I learned a lot." He waved to his pictures. "Like these."

He shrugged and waved at still another tourist he must know. "There's a lot of birch bark going to waste in those woods and I have a rather expensive chunk of Minnesota wilderness to pay for and every penny counts."

He couldn't keep the tiny tinge of bitterness from his voice. The comparison between the two of them. All she had to do to own considerably more acres than he was purchasing was to get a job and live the old way for a year. Just one year. He was doing all kinds of things to pay for his property.

Speaking of jobs, if Bruce knew as many people as he seemed to know, he might be a wonderful source of information, might know of a job. But, as she was framing her request for information, a large family group descended on the booth and she wisely gave them room because, if they wanted to buy something Bruce had to sell, she'd best let them shop to their heart's content.

And so it went for the remainder of the afternoon until she decided to give up on talking further with Bruce, waved goodbye to him over the heads of a couple people buying three of his birch bark pictures, bought her groceries at the local supermarket, and drove as fast as she dared along the highway and then very, very slowly and carefully down the driveway until she reached her house and filled the cupboards with enough staples that she shouldn't have to make the trip again for a very long time. Her car would thank her.

Not long after stowing everything away, but before evening arrived, a truck turned into her driveway. Bruce jumped out and she met him at the door along with a tail-wagging, chest thumping London who would have knocked him over if Bruce hadn't been prepared for the onslaught. "Hey, guy, how're you doing? Keeping Abby safe from bears and other dangers?" He wrestled with the dog for a moment before entering the house. "Just curious as to how you're doing." He glanced about the kitchen, not quite as spic and span as during his first visit but plenty clean enough for anyone with limited access to hot water. "I see you're still abiding by rules that were never clearly laid out and probably aren't half as severe as you think."

"I'm taking no chances." What if Grandma Maude decided she was living too free a lifestyle? What if she decided Abby didn't deserve the place? What would Abby do then? Return to Minneapolis and look for another job selling expensive dresses to wealthy women? No! It was a great first job but not the career she wanted. "I'll do whatever it takes to stay here."

Bruce sucked in his breath and poured himself a glass of water, which caused Abby to wince. "You mean you're not even drinking water from the kitchen?"

"It might not be allowed."

Her frowned. "Well water is safer for human consumption than lake water."

"I know that but – but --."

"But you're drinking lake water anyway?" He wiped his mouth with his sleeve. "I hope you're using tablets to make sure it's safe."

Her expression said she'd not thought of that but she had an answer. "Pioneers didn't have tablets."

"Pioneers didn't worry about contamination from the river that comes into the lake." He couldn't believe she hadn't bought tablets. "Farm runoff. Fishermen dropping all sorts of stuff in the lakes. Who knows what all is in that water."

She sagged. "I'll get some tablets next time I go to town."

"Or just use water from the tap. I doubt your grandmother would want you to risk death or disease." He looked about the kitchen. "Do you use lake water for cooking?" Her expression said she did. "Remind me not to eat here, though I was going to suggest we pick some more strawberries and make more of those mouth-watering muffins and eat them on the deck and watch the fish jump in the lake."

She wilted. "I'll use tap water until I can get some tablets."

"Smart girl. Smarter would be to call your grandmother and get a few things straightened out. But, hey, tap water for muffins is a start even if they use milk instead of water. You wash the dishes in water and, since I'm sure you ignore that beautiful, modern, time-saving dishwasher, I doubt that your wash water has been boiled."

She sank further into herself, wondering if she'd get sick or die, seeking the first faint stirrings of a water-borne illness inside of herself and glad to find nothing. Yet. "We can wash the dishes first."

"Good thinking." He hitched himself onto the counter. "And now what say we go pick strawberries? Or I can pick them while you wash dishes and yourself and the kitchen counter."

They did as he suggested and by the time the sun turned the lake into an orange-red carpet spread before them, they were enjoying muffins and cold cuts from town that Abby was sure were healthy and not contaminated with any unseen poisons.

Bruce gave a contented sigh. "I thank you for washing the dishes. No sense in taking chances. The first thing I did when I bought the adjoining property was to have the water tested and was glad to learn that it's healthy though it tastes like crap."

"Iron." Abby's grandfather had insisted on a the most advanced water conditioner available and, as a result, the cabin water was as good and as good tasting as any from a bottle and now that she thought about it, Bruce was probably right about her grandmother not wanting her to put her health at risk. "Maybe I will start using the kitchen water. But not the dishwasher."

"Not yet, huh?" He sighed mightily. "If I had a dishwasher I'd use it all the time and yours isn't just a dishwasher, it's the best one around. Like the stove that could be used to cook for an army. I'm envious as heck and sure that your grandmother will agree that they should be used."

He turned to consider her. Swept her from head to toe, taking in the designer jeans and frilly blouse she'd worn to town. Sent frissons down her spine even without touching her, which was a first. She didn't normally react to the male sex so forcefully and he hadn't even touched her but there was still electricity.

43

"Which makes me wonder if you use the fabulous, does-everything-except-fold-the-clothes-and-put-them-away washing machine and dryer that I suspect are in that laundry off the kitchen. Because, if you use lake water and wash everything on a washboard, which is a thing of torture and don't ask how I know because the memory is too painful to recount – if you use lake water, then all those pretty and very expensive designer clothes will turn orange from rust and lose that soft, clingy quality that looks so good on you."

Abby groaned and dropped her head to hide an unexpected blush. "What else did pioneers do that you know all about?"

He laughed, a comfortable sound that echoed the evening birdsong and bounced off the walls. "A lot but those will do for starters."

Abby groaned a second time. "You make a good point but I'm stymied. I don't know what I can and can't do but I don't want to lose this place because I'm being too lazy and not living in the old way."

"Hmmmmm." He munched on a muffin and took a swig of healthy, pollutant free water from the kitchen sink with ice cubes that came from the state-of-the-art refrigerator's ice maker. "So do what I suggested. Call. Today. Now. If she cares about you – if she wants you to have this place – she'll at least give some guidance."

"I suppose I could do that." In a very small voice. "But it'll be hard because I don't want to do anything to make her change her mind." She sat up straight and found it suddenly hard to talk. To say what she was thinking. Because it meant so much, was so important. "I want this place. I want it badly."

He softened. "Of course you do. You're sitting on a

slice of paradise, not to mention a fortune in real estate. But think about it. Anyone who'd give all this away must care enough to want it to go to someone who will love and cherish it." He leaned towards her. "Am I right? Does that describe your grandmother?"

"Yes, but I don't want to take any chances. She was pretty firm about the conditions."

"That she didn't lay out in detail." His expression said that was a very odd thing.

"My cousins asked her for details but she refused and then they said they didn't want the place no matter what the conditions were if it would mean giving up their fantastic jobs. They said so at least a dozen times and because they love their jobs they tried to get her to change the condition that it become a permanent residence. She was firm about that, though, so in the end I was the only one who wanted the property."

Bruce was silent for a long time. When he spoke, it was in an odd voice and she couldn't begin to imagine what he was thinking. "Your cousins didn't jump at the chance to own a piece of real estate that's worth a fortune no matter what the conditions were?" When Abby shook her head, he added, "How rich is your family, anyway?" Then he added quickly, "Not that you have to tell me, not specifically, because I don't mean to pry. It's just hard for me to fathom anyone passing this place up in favor of a job no matter how great unless that person has more money than I can imagine in my wildest dreams."

His comment brought Abby up short and made her consider her family "We aren't rich, not like some people. But, yes, I suppose we are comfortable."

A noise in Bruce's throat said what he thought of

her terminology, but he didn't pursue the idea and soon was slathering another muffin with butter she'd bought in town earlier and showing her what he'd brought home from the craft show. The birch-bark pictures that didn't sell. He held one against the kitchen wall where it set off the earthenware pottery on a nearby shelf. "Want it? It'll look nice here."

She accepted the picture and promised to contact her grandmother and he left after hugging London a few dozen times and making sure that all the strawberries currently ripe were in a basket in the kitchen sink where they would be cleaned with safe, cold well water before being put in the freezer. He waved before climbing into his truck that had high enough clearance for the worst the driveway could throw at it and disappeared down that driveway, bouncing as he went. A year previous, Abby would have laughed at his truck. Now she envied him.

CHAPTER 5

Abby didn't sleep well that night and spent many hours staring at nothing because getting a job in Johns Falls wasn't going to be easy but would be essential if she wanted to ever own the property she'd long ago come to love. The one thing that had been made clear during her phone conversation with her grandmother was that 'the old way' didn't involve anything that put her health at risk and that of course she could use every convenience in the house as long as she didn't hold wild parties or do other wanton things.

At the same time, she made it very clear that the condition of becoming a permanent resident wasn't negotiable so she shouldn't even ask and, unless she was independently wealthy, which she wasn't in spite of what Bruce seemed to think, that meant finding a source of income.

She didn't tell her grandmother that getting a job wasn't looking too good at the moment so the thought of employment – or lack of it -- kept her awake and as long as she couldn't sleep, she decided she might as well watch the moonlight cross her bedroom ceiling until she finally came up with a plan. A desperate plan but one that just might work if she went about it right.

She'd convince every business in town to accept her application and tell them that she'd be available as soon as the high school and college kids they'd hired for the summer quit. It wouldn't provide her with a job immediately but might just give her what she needed by the time autumn arrived. She had minimal savings to get her by until then.

It would work because student help was temporary. She'd worked summers while going to school, surely there were kids in Johns Falls doing the same thing. So having decided, she slept well at last and woke with the sun. Way too early but good experience for when she'd have a job and would need to get ready for work.

She soon decided that she was more than grateful for the water that gushed from the kitchen tap, both hot and cold, and as soon as she'd had a hearty breakfast cooked on the wonderful stove, she cleaned and cleaned and cleaned until the house sparkled. Then she took a long, hot shower and realized for the first time in her life what a luxury it was. Then she poured herself a glass of lemonade, called London to join her, sat on the deck overlooking the lake and put her feet on a second chair with London at her feet and simply enjoyed being alive.

Until she heard the unmistakable sound of Bruce's truck bumping along the driveway and soon after that the sound of two very large dogs running headlong to the deck where she and London were relaxing and soon

London was off and running with Paris and Madrid while Bruce found himself a glass of lemonade from the kitchen and then found another chair and pulled it alongside hers.

"Did you call your grandmother yet?"

"You're pretty nosy but, yes I did and she agreed with you about health concerns so I'm using hot and cold running water and the dishwasher and everything else."

"Everything?"

"Pure luxury." Which made her curious. "Almost up to your standards?"

He sighed. "My water is safe but it's only hot once a day because I turn on the generator for a couple hours while I do my medical billing and make dinner and while I'm working the water gets hot. But when I'm done and have had a hot dinner and washed the dishes in hot water and had a hot shower, then the generator goes off for another day. And, yes, those few hours of hot water are pure luxury."

"No electricity except for a few hours?" He shook his head. "Why not if you have a generator?"

"Because it's a lot smaller than yours and I don't want to wear it out." She considered that information and wanted to ask more questions but thought better of it because it was beginning to look as if Bruce was living close to the way she'd originally expected to live and he wasn't exactly happy about it.

His next words told her that she was right. "I live in a shack I built in a week. It's not much but it's weather tight and keeps me warm in the winter and is comfortable and electricity a few hours a day works because I'm alone and I grew up with no electricity at all until my parents had it installed so I'm pretty self-sufficient at all the things you think you should be doing that you shouldn't because you'll get yourself killed and I'm so glad your grandmother agreed."

"How did your parents come to live the way they do?"

"They were college professors who decided to go back to the land and live without modern conveniences, to live as your grandmother did while young, except my parents did so voluntarily instead of because nothing else was available. Then they had me, and the rest is history."

He stopped for a moment, remembering, then continued, "I plan on having every luxury known to mankind as soon as I can afford them but, meanwhile, I know how to subsist on very little and I'm glad because it enables me to pay off my mortgage early, after which I'll build a house with every luxury you already have."

"Oh my goodness." Abby couldn't think of a single other thing to say and stared at Bruce openmouthed until she realized what she was doing and shut it with a snap.

He wasn't finished. "And, speaking of making a few bucks, how do you plan to make a living here in the wilderness unless your grandmother changed her mind about you making a living here?"

She told him of her conversation with her grandmother that ended with that being the one absolute condition. Then she told him of her disappointing job search and he nodded and said it was what he'd expected. "But there will be jobs, there always are. Eventually. Probably. Hopefully. Maybe."

She groaned as he stopped long enough to pet three

dogs that had bounded onto the deck and were jumping all over him before dashing away once more and scrambling down to the lake where they jumped into the water with huge splashes and swam for a few moments before coming back to the deck where they shook themselves all over Abby and Bruce. Then he continued as if they weren't both sopping wet. "I don't believe the problem will be finding a job." He shook his head in the most depressing way. "No, the problem will be getting to it in the winter when the driveway is impassable."

"I'll have it plowed."

"Good luck with that because it's so awful that no plow driver I've spoken to will endanger their expensive equipment on that disaster that someone laughingly called a driveway."

"My grandfather built houses, not driveways." Which was beginning to look like a real problem. "And I can't afford to have someone rebuild it."

He sighed in what sounded like relief. "I'm glad to hear that because I've been losing sleep over how I'd manage to pay my half of having a new driveway put in."

"It's a shared driveway." She'd forgotten about that and now that she knew he was just as broke as she was with her meagre savings disappearing rapidly, she knew that the driveway would just have to stay as it was. "But I'll get to work somehow. I will. When I get a job."

They were silent for a while, and then Bruce shrugged his shoulders. "There will be a way, there always is. In the meantime, I passed your garden on the way here and why haven't you been picking the strawberries?"

"We picked them when you were here last."

He rolled his eyes. "Do I have to teach you everything? Was your upbringing so incomplete that you don't even know that plants in gardens ripen continually and, thus there are now more strawberries to be picked?" He looked at her hopefully. "And turned into more delicious muffins?"

She reddened and wished she'd stop making newbie gaffes, but soon they were in the garden with buckets that were surprisingly close to full when they returned to the kitchen. "But I still have berries in the freezer. There will be a whole lot of extra berries."

"We can add what's left of these to the freezer when we are done." He was already pulling ingredients from the cupboards and turning on the oven because he'd helped before and knew what was needed and where things were located.

She shook her head. "The freezer is full. I had to move stuff around to add the berries from last week and I don't know what to do with the berries that aren't quite ripe yet but will be soon."

He rubbed the back of his neck. "There are also blueberries and raspberries in the garden and I saw some hazelnut bushes on my way here and they make great muffins too and my cheapskate soul can't stand the thought of them rotting away."

"I can't see buying another freezer." What did freezers cost, anyway? She didn't have a clue and didn't want to have to find out.

"I have an idea."

"I could use an idea about now." As long as it didn't involve her inexperience in the forest.

It didn't. "Do you enjoy baking muffins?"

She thought about it. Yes, she did. She and her grandmother had had great times covering these very kitchen counters with flour and throwing berries at each other until they had to stop if they wanted enough berries left for muffins. "Yes, I enjoy baking."

"Then use all these berries, both the ones that are fresh and the ones in the freezer and bake your little heart out until you have a whole lot of muffins. Then take them to the farmers' market this coming weekend and sell them. Earn a little money."

"Me? Sell food at an outdoor market?" She shook her head in horror. "I don't know how to sell." Unlike Bruce who clearly could sell refrigerators to Eskimos and knew everyone in town and every tourist who'd ever visited Johns Falls. The man was awesome and she'd never be able to do what he did. "I'd look like a fool."

"Then you'll be in good company. Being willing to make a fool of oneself is an essential part of selling anything."

She couldn't do it. Couldn't. "But I don't have one of those white tents everyone uses."

"No problem. I have two. Three, to be exact, but we each only need one and I'll be glad to help put one of them up for you." He found bowls and looked for the card with the muffin recipe. Abby got it for him and together they began making muffins. "You can set up beside me, I'll help in any way possible, and I know that you'll be the hit of the market. I guarantee it."

Bruce didn't speak again until the muffins were in the oven and they'd poured themselves still more lemonade to drink while waiting for them to be done.

"I'll pick you up right after sunup on Saturday. So have your muffins packed and ready, as many as you have berries for."

When the muffins were finished and they'd eaten enough to not want to look at another muffin again – ever – he said goodbye to London and Abby, in that order and she noticed that he spent more time ruffling the dog's head than he did talking to her. Which was probably good because that tiny shock she felt whenever he touched her – that was surely a residual of the bear encounter -- hadn't gone away yet. Was increasing, if such was possible.

Paris and Madrid leaped into the back of his pickup, he climbed into the cab and was gone and the place was as quiet as before he'd come. Too quiet. Abby was growing used to his presence and the commotion of three dogs chasing each other everywhere.

She found that she was restless, thinking over what he'd said. She had to do something, move, jump, anything. So she went to the garden to estimate how many berries were likely to ripen in time for the weekend. Then she went into the kitchen and wondered if she should head for town at once to purchase extra muffin tins or wait until tomorrow. She decided to wait until morning because it was growing late and she didn't want to come home in the dark and have to navigate the driveway blind. She'd probably break an axle.

Then she used the wonderful stove her grandfather had insisted was essential for extended family get-togethers to cook a dinner that wasn't out of a can and she enjoyed every single bite while wondering how much money could be made selling muffins at a local farmers' market. If any.

CHAPTER 6

The next day was spent buying several muffin tins plus a whole lot of flour and other ingredients, picking the few strawberries in the garden that had ripened over-night, and strategizing how to bake a whole lot of strawberry muffins, wrap them neatly and nicely, and pack them so they'd arrive intact and stay that way for the several hours that the market would be open and then bring the leftovers home because there'd surely be a lot of those. Then she made a second trip to town because she might need paper bags to put them in if someone bought some. Which they probably wouldn't.

Then she got to work. Forgot to enjoy the beauty of the day until London nosed her towards the deck and a few minutes of outdoor play. That required cleaning herself and her clothes before getting flour all over everything so baking took longer than it might have.

She took a walk to the lake and along the shore because London thought it was a good idea to get some exercise. Didn't meet any bears or other denizens of the forest but picked a bouquet of yellow wildflowers that fit perfectly in an old, cracked vase that she remembered as being somewhere in the kitchen cupboards.

She returned home in time for a snack that both she and London enjoyed on the deck, after which London stayed outside to run off some of his energy and protect her home from any stray bears that might take it into their heads to come visiting, and she got more muffins baked, wrapped, and in the freezer because she wasn't sure they'd stay fresh until the weekend if she left them on the counter.

Saturday morning, she set her alarm, something she'd not done since quitting her sales job, and was ready and waiting when Bruce pulled up in his truck, the back of which was filled with two white canopies and folded tables and other things she couldn't imagine the purpose of. He carefully placed the boxes of muffins in an empty space that he'd obviously left just for them, shoving aside a few boxes of his own to make more room because she'd made more muffins than even Bruce had thought possible.

They set off for town, moving slowly along the deeply rutted driveway so as not to disturb anything in the pickup's bed, then as fast as the law allowed once reaching the highway. They arrived at the farmers' market in time to see a couple other people already setting up canopies. "Is this all that will be here?"

He chuckled, a low, warm sound. "No, but it's first come first served for places to set up and I wanted to get good spots for both of us."

It took only minutes to erect the canopies by shoving parts wherever they needed shoving as Bruce demonstrated and clicking locks whenever they needed clicking and driving stakes into the ground to hold everything safe in case of sudden, unexpected wind gusts. Then Bruce dragged the folding tables from the pickup and instructed Abby as to their erection so she found herself unfolding them and once again shoving and clicking away while he carried all the boxes from the pickup to their spots as more and still more vendors arrived and began doing the exact same thing in their own, less valuable, spots because they'd arrived too late to get the best ones.

Abby was glad Bruce was next to her. For one thing, she'd not thought to have money for making change which proved essential as soon as the first people strolled through because almost every single visitor wanted muffins and, without Bruce nearby with a lot of change, she'd not have been able to sell anything because she'd not have been able to make change. But Bruce simply said to keep track of how many muffins she sold and they'd figure things out at the end of the day. He then pulled a notebook from his back pocket along with a pen for her to keep track of muffins and she didn't know whether to laugh or cry at her abysmal lack of business smarts.

"You'll learn."

"If there's any reason to learn because, if I bring home as many muffins as I brought, there won't be any reason to come again." Bruce was about to say he doubted that would be the case but she never knew for sure because an elderly couple who hadn't yet had breakfast bought four muffins to munch on while perusing everything else that was for sale. Like Bruce's pictures which they liked enough to buy one.

When the couple had made the rounds, they returned to Abby's booth and bought a half dozen more muffins to take home. "These are wonderful."

"My grandmother's recipe," was all Abby could think to say, wondering if she'd ever develop Bruce's gift of gab.

"Your grandmother? Wonderful. That's why they are so good. Old recipes are always the best."

Abby agreed, put their purchases in one of the paper bags as she silently gave thanks for at least remembering to have on hand – one thing out of a dozen essentials to selling at an outdoor market -- then turned to the next couple, a young man and his very pregnant wife with a toddler in tow, who bought three muffins and they, too, returned before leaving to buy a full dozen to take home.

"Looks like your muffins are a hit."

Abby was cautious. "It's early. People are buying them for breakfast. Maybe they won't sell so well later in the day."

But they did. Shortly after a hasty lunch eaten on her feet while waiting on customers, someone else stopped by her booth. She smiled the bright smile copied from Bruce, who never seemed to tire of talking to people and who never, ever frowned. And waited for the man before her to say what he wanted.

He wanted a muffin, just one, and he unwrapped and ate it right there. Tipped his head. Smiled a very small but very real smile. And spoke. "How'd you like to make muffins for my restaurant? I could use something this good for the breakfast crowd. And cupcakes for later, if you do those, too."

She didn't know what to say. Stood there with her

mouth open feeling like an idiot. Bruce, who'd heard the exchange, came to her rescue. "Hey, Mickey, I'm her next-door neighbor and I say she can and will if the details can be worked out." He patted Abby's shoulder but she managed to ignore the electric shock this time in order to pay attention to the stranger. Mickey. "She's pretty busy, of course, because her muffins are the best and most wonderful muffins in the world, but she can possibly work you into her schedule."

Mickey harrumphed that she couldn't be all that busy if she was selling at a farmers' market instead being in her kitchen making muffins for all of her customers. Then he went around the table to where Bruce stood and the two embraced in the kind of hug men favored, all thumping and pumping and generally acting like London, Paris and Madrid at play.

When Mickey left, Bruce waited until he was out of sight, then jumped over a table to give Abby an electric hug and waltz her around her booth as much as was possible in such a small space. "You've got a customer, Abby. A real customer. You're on your way."

Abby was full of questions. "How many should I make? When should I deliver them? Are they wrapped right?"

He shushed her. "All will be determined in good time." He looked at the sun and then at her almost depleted supply of muffins. "We'll go talk to him as soon as the market closes or you run out of product, whichever happens first and I suspect you'll run out of muffins in a half hour or so."

Which proved to be true. Less than an hour later, she sold her last muffin and started packing up her booth, reversing the shoving and clicking she'd done to set up the booth earlier that morning. Bruce wasn't sold out but he proceeded to take down his display also. "You still have things to sell."

"You heard me, didn't you? I'm your neighbor and temporary business manager until you figure out how to do it yourself – meaning I know Mickey and I seem to know more about the world of small-town businesses than you do – so I'm going with you." He waved to his unsold works of art. "Don't worry, they won't melt and I can sell them next time."

So, eventually, the pickup truck was gunned and pointed towards Mickey's Pub and Eatery on the shore of the river that originated in the lake beside which Bruce and Abby lived before meandering through the forest and the town of Johns Falls and over the falls that gave the town its name, and then beyond, passing Mickey's on its way towards the larger north woods and, eventually, Lake Superior.

Mickey's turned out to be a lovely log building with huge windows overlooking the river and a fireplace in the center of the large dining room that was always lit, even in the middle of summer, necessitating air conditioning so his customers didn't overheat.

Mickey placed a small order – a dozen muffins and an equal number of cupcakes – and informed Abby that if they went over as well as he expected, his next order would be for way more.

Abby didn't think the strawberry garden would produce a huge order, not even if she added to the number with wild ones from the patch where she'd encountered a bear and the thought of going back there made her pause a moment until she realized that

London would be with her to warn her of any imminent bear attacks. But there still wouldn't be enough berries and what about when the strawberry season ended? She opened her mouth to say something when Bruce kicked her under the table they were seated around so she shut up.

Bruce took over the conversation, giving Mickey his best business type look. "She'll keep you supplied with muffins. Don't worry about a thing."

Mickey nodded and they prepared to leave, when Mickey put a hand on Abby's arm to hold her back. "I just thought of something. You do make your muffins and cupcakes in a commercial kitchen, don't you? Because if you make them in your home, I can't use them. It's against the law."

She wilted and was about to say the deal would have to be off when Bruce grabbed her arm and gave it good, hard squeeze and took over the conversation once again. "Of course she does. Wouldn't do it any other way." Micky nodded and they left the building.

"Why did you say that? I don't have a commercial kitchen so I can't provide him with anything."

Bruce hustled her to the truck where they could talk without Mickey hearing. "I know that but I also know the town of Johns Falls. Surely there's a commercial kitchen somewhere in town that you can use." He smiled fatuously. "Until you can build your own and get rich baking muffins and cupcakes." He stopped smiling. "You can bake cupcakes, can't you?"

"I suppose so. They are pretty similar to muffins but my grandmother never mentioned any wonderful, fabulous recipes."

"Call her. Ask is she knows of any scrumptious

cupcake recipes."

Abby promised to do so as soon as she got home and had a chance to come down from the excitement of her first day selling strawberry muffins. And she did, that evening after making sure the time difference wouldn't mean her grandmother would be asleep. And, yes, Maude did know a few pretty good recipes for cupcakes that she'd made as a kid because as long as they'd had the muffin tins they might as well make good use of them.

Before an hour had passed, Grandma Maude had emailed half a dozen cupcake recipes that Abby was sure would be as wonderful as the muffins. Now if Bruce knew what he was talking about and could find her a commercial kitchen in Johns Falls, she'd be set up nicely to make a few dollars.

Of course, muffins and cupcakes weren't a living, not like a real job, but now that she thought about it, being in town to bake and make deliveries would help her meet business owners and that could result in the job that she so badly needed if she was going to become a permanent resident of the Johns Falls area.

CHAPTER 7

The next morning, Sunday, Abby woke to the sound of Bruce's truck bumping and banging its way to her place. She jumped up, pulled on clothes and shoved her feet into sneakers in time to make it to the door before he knocked. Looked through the door and decided she must be underdressed because he wore fairly new, clean jeans and a shirt that wasn't his usual tee shirt with a couple holes in it.

"Hey, it's Sunday. Church." He looked her up and down. "Unless you don't go to church though I know your grandma Maude did. We usually went together so I figured you and I might do the same. Save on gas." He took a step back and prepared to return to his truck. "Sorry if I thought wrong."

"No. Wait. I do go to church. That is I will go except I've not been to church here in Johns Falls since I was a kid." Looked down at her well-worn clothes. "Give me a second to change." Looked at the clock on the wall. "Do I have time?"

He relented, came back, dropped into a chair on the deck. "If you hurry."

"I promise." And she raced back to her bedroom thinking all the way what to wear to church in Johns Falls, Minnesota. Remembered what Bruce was wearing. Pulled out a brand-new pair of semi-dressy jeans she'd thought would be appropriate for roughing it in the wilderness until she got there and realized the flimsy material would be torn to pieces in five minutes of walking through the underbrush. But they would be perfect for church, with a pink, puffy blouse over them and a pair of sandals.

She ran back to where Bruce waited, raking fingers through her hair as she ran and wondering why she wore it long instead of getting it cut. Short enough not to tangle in that same underbrush that would turn her dressy jeans to tatters would be practical. But it was too late now, she'd have to do the best she could and maybe she could wear braids in the forest.

Bruce whistled when he saw her. "That was fast. And you look like a million dollars." Examined her more leisurely, up and down, hair and all. "More than a million."

On the way to church, he talked. "There's an ulterior motive for going to church today. After church, I want you to meet a friend of mine, Carolyn Keen, who happens to own a commercial kitchen that she's not using at the moment. At least I don't think she is because she used to supply Mickey with pies and I didn't notice any when we were there yesterday. So it's a possibility and might be why he wants cupcakes. Because he no longer has Carolyn's pies."

She flicked sidewise looks at Bruce during the drive to the smallish church on the edge of town. He cleaned up well, she decided. She'd never seen him dressed up before and, though what they were both wearing couldn't remotely be called dressy if they were in any city at all, they were slightly more formal than what the mother bear and its cubs had seen that day in the strawberry patch.

Yes, he definitely looked nice – she couldn't quite figure out what part of him she liked the most because he was truly male from head to toe -- and after a quick perusal, she turned to the window to examine the passing scenery because looking at him was doing something to her insides and the last thing she needed – wanted -- right now was to feel what she was feeling. Because she had things to do. Commitments to meet. A house to earn. A job to find.

Abby drew in a breath. "Do you think your friend will let me use her kitchen?"

"For a small fee, probably, and she'll be in church today unless she's at death's door."

Abby spent the whole service wondering what 'a small fee' would consist of and whether she could afford it and looking about the church to see if she was over or under dressed. It turned out that she fit in with everyone else thanks to checking out what Bruce was wearing when he stopped to pick her up.

Figuring out at last that this former backwoodsman who lived in a shack in the forest knew his way around the social aspects of life in Johns Falls, she gave herself up to being dragged by him to the fellowship hall after the service where she found herself with coffee and cookies and introductions to all kinds of people she didn't know from Adam but who had known Grandma Maude and, therefore were so glad she'd come to live in Johns Falls. Or who knew Bruce and, since he'd brought her, figured that she was a totally nice person or he wouldn't have bothered with her, never mind that they were next door neighbors and coming together was a practical decision.

Then he introduced her to an elderly woman named Carolyn Keen. Abby took a deep breath and wondered what to say to the woman who owned a commercial kitchen and could make or break her immediate future. The future that could make all the difference financially. Could determine whether she could afford trips to town for food and other essentials of life or whether her tiny savings would be gone by the time she found a real job. She'd been surprised at how much she'd made selling muffins. If an agreement could be reached, her immediate future would be taken care of.

Carolyn Keen was a nice lady, that was the first thing Abby noticed, who remembered Grandma Maude though she was a bit younger than Abby's grandmother and so hadn't been in the same grade. "But we went on field trips together and were both on the cheerleading squad, though at different times."

Mrs. Keen, widowed for several years, gave Abby the same hug that practically everyone else in church had given her after Bruce introduced her. The elderly lady didn't act as though she knew Bruce was maneuvering her towards a corner table for some reason she couldn't fathom though she surely did know he was doing it because her eyes were sharp and intelligent and full of questions as she dropped into a chair and put her coffee and cookies on the table and stared at him and waited.

He didn't keep her waiting long. "You still have that commercial kitchen?"

She nodded, giving him a slightly incredulous stare. "I've tried to sell it and all kinds of people want the building but not the equipment that's inside and what would I do with all that expensive stuff? Let it sit outside and rust? I don't think so. So, yes, I still have it. Why? Don't tell me you've decided to bake pies for a living?"

"Noooo." He scratched his head and Abby realized that this man who seemed to know everyone and everything about Johns Falls wasn't sure how to explain what he wanted. "Not me." He hesitantly put a hand on Abby's shoulder. It was warm and solid and reassuring, which was probably his intent, and sent electricity throughout her body, which probably wasn't intentional. "Abby, here, is the baker and she doesn't make pies, she bakes muffins and Mickey is interested but they must be baked in a commercial kitchen and she doesn't have one." He became suddenly anxious. "You don't use your kitchen any more, do you?"

The elderly Carolyn Keen blinked in an effort to take in what Bruce was saying. Thought a moment silently. Blinked again to let them know that she'd figured it out but that she realized there was more to be said. And waited.

At which point Abbey realized something. The muffins were her muffins and she was the one who needed the kitchen. If she was going to stand on her own two feet, to find a job and make her own way in Johns Falls, to become self-sufficient as per her grandmother's wishes, then she shouldn't let Bruce drag her around like a little kid and do her talking for her. So she looked Carolyn Keen in the eye and explained about the muffins and Mickey's and her need for a commercial kitchen if one was available.

Carolyn Keen's response was to smile broadly and for a long time, the smile growing wider with each passing second, until she came around the table and hugged Abby for a second time. "You are the answer to my prayers. Someone who'll use that white elephant of a kitchen and keep all that expensive equipment from falling into decay and disrepair until I can sell it and don't worry, we'll figure out a rent that'll work for both of us."

Abby sagged in relief. With just a little luck, this was going to work and she'd at least make a few dollars to keep her going until a job opened up, which, judging from the lack of 'help wanted' signs, could be quite a while. She didn't know anything about commercial kitchens – hadn't even known there was such a thing – and so wasn't sure how the whole commercial-kitchen thing worked.

But she smiled and smiled and smiled and decided to worry about the details later, when she was sitting on her deck overlooking the lake with a glass of iced tea in one hand and her laptop on her lap as she learned everything she didn't yet know but could surely learn online about the commercial food industry.

Meanwhile, Carolyn was thinking a mile a minute, frowning. "If you don't have your Kitchen Manager's license yet, I can fill in for that because the kitchen is next to my house so I can pop over when necessary."

"Kitchen Manager's license?" Abby was clearly dumbfounded. "What's that?"

Carolyn blew out through her nose and didn't laugh. "A commercial kitchen requires a kitchen manager on the premises to make sure everything is done properly." Seeing Abby's very confused expression, she continued. "Don't worry, it's easy enough to get a license. Just take a government course online and wait for the certificate to come in the mail and I'll stick around until it arrives."

Abby sagged. "This is more complicated than I thought."

Bruce slipped an arm around her shoulders. More electricity but he was warm and solid and she liked that as he said, "But worth it if it'll give you a business that'll provide the income required to live in Johns Falls." She didn't say that it would be a temporary solution to a very long-term problem, but she thought it. Carolyn and Bruce were both nice to help out and she appreciated that. But a long-term solution? Not a few muffins. She'd still need that job, but time was now on her side.

Carolyn finished her coffee and cookies and suggested they follow her to her house because the kitchen was next door and they could look it over and make sure it would meet Abby's requirements, though Abby hadn't a clue what those were. But the visit was expected and so she and Bruce went to his truck while she wished she had her laptop so she could learn at least a few fundamentals about commercial food service before deciding whether the kitchen would do.

It was a surprisingly small building but it was clean and had all the usual kitchen things in larger, commercial sizes and some of them were different from what was in her kitchen but even a newcomer like Abby could figure them out. And they had user manuals.

There were a lot of pie pans because Carolyn Keen had made pies and no muffin tins but that was easily remedied. Abby found herself nodding and signing a rental agreement that would take a minimal percentage of the proceeds, which meant that she should still be able to make a profit.

Carolyn explained. "If you don't make money, then you won't use the kitchen for long and I'll be back where I was before you came along. So I want you to make a profit." And, as Bruce explained later as they were bumping along the driveway towards the lake, Carolyn had been selling pies to Mickeys and other places long enough to know how much rent to charge. And Carolyn had told them what to charge Mickey for the muffins.

Abby nodded without hearing a word, on automatic because her mind was a million miles away, on commercial kitchens and kitchen manager's licenses and rental percentages and other things she'd not imagined in her wildest dreams that she'd be considering when she went to the farmers' market the previous day.

As Bruce started away, she almost stopped him to offer him iced tea or lemonade because that was a habit they'd sort of gotten into but, as she raised her arm to beckon him back, he shook his head as if he knew what she was going through and how confused she was and he headed into the forest and his home because she needed this time to herself.

CHAPTER 8

The next morning Bruce woke up to birdsong and thoughts of Abby. His next door neighbor. The smallish woman with brown hair streaked blonde here and there in what could be natural but was more likely the result of a very expensive stylist. She was cute as a button, obviously came from money – hence the well-done blonde streaks -- and didn't have a clue about wilderness life. Or how to make a living away from cities. Probably had never had to work for a paycheck until now and why the nice, practical, grandmotherly woman he'd met when he bought his own place put restrictions on Abby getting title to property was -- odd.

Someday the grandmother would visit and he'd ask her. Privately, of course. But now he merely rolled over, wished the birds would shut up, and closed his eyes for a few more winks while deciding that maybe Maude had a good reason. He'd give her the benefit of the doubt.

The birds ignored his wishes, growing louder with every passing moment until he finally heaved himself upright and looked longingly at the coffee pot that hadn't yet learned how to make coffee without his input. Someday he'd have one that did, that he could set the night before to have coffee ready when he awoke, the kind Abby had probably left behind when she moved to the forest. The kind that might be somewhere in the kitchen cupboards of the house she lived in now. He made a note to himself to find out the next time he was there. He really liked coffee.

It took him a while to make coffee and drink a few cups while finding some leftover rolls for breakfast, so Abby was up and heading for her car when he pulled his truck beside it and jumped out and why he'd decided to do a good deed that involved her was more than he could figure this early in the morning, but here he was, ready to be helpful and oddly glad he was here. Smiling. Happy for her if the day went right. "Why don't we ride together and save the shocks on that tiny car of yours?"

She couldn't imagine why he was there. "Are you going to town?"

"We need to clean the kitchen."

Oops. Yes, it hadn't been used in a while and needed cleaning. She hadn't thought of that. "You don't have to help."

"Yes, I do." He sighed and wondered if those noisy birds were even now laughing themselves silly for waking him up this morning because, if they'd have let him sleep just a few minutes longer, Abby would be gone and he'd have returned home and put his feet up with a clear conscience. But they hadn't and now he was here and committed to helping her. "This whole thing was my idea. I want to see how it turns out."

Abby hesitated, biting her lip and trying to decide how much help was acceptable and, more to the point, whether she should accept help at all. Whether help would negate her agreement with Grandma Maude.

She bit her lip again and Bruce rolled his eyes. "Oh, come on, don't quibble. I can wipe down a counter with the best of them and it'll get done in half the time with two people working and I'm not busy today." He truly didn't have anything that absolutely had to be done in the next few hours. He could split wood any time and was caught up on the medical billing until tomorrow. She he wasn't lying. Quite.

She flushed and got into his truck, dropping cleaning supplies behind the seat as he left the yard and asked, "Got a list? There will be things you'll need." She flashed a notebook with a list already started.

They set off for town and as he drove she wondered, not for the first time, how he avoided the bumps and ruts and still got to the highway in half the time it took her and did so without damaging his truck's shocks. She'd ask him some time; the knowledge would be useful when she started commuting to the commercial kitchen on a regular basis and just the thought that she'd be doing such a business-like thing as commuting gave her a tiny thrill because it meant that she was getting a handle on her new life and that meant the possibility of owning the house in the forest was greater than ever.

She was on her way to -- something. Financial security? Selling enough muffins to keep her going until she got a job? All of the above? As the truck neared the highway, she wondered at how her life was so different from what she'd expected just a few short weeks earlier.

Bruce watched her from the corner of his eye. She was thinking about something, that was clear from her determined expression, and he wondered what it was. Muffins? The trees that flashed quickly by once they reached the highway and picked up speed? Him, Bruce Merriweather? Was she thinking about him? Could she be thinking about him?

Of course not, and he was an idiot to even consider such an idea and couldn't imagine why he had such a thought. He was a useful resource person who was helping her own a piece of excellent property but he was totally unimportant to her life plan and that thought caused him to fall into a bout of depression that made him fiercely aware of the sun turning her light brown hair into a halo of spun gold that cascaded down her back and her blue eyes into the gentians his mother had planted beside their house when he was a kid. The house that would probably fit in Abby's living room.

She turned towards him, tipping her head until her hair flew about her head in an even brighter goldish haze while her eyes echoed the shine of the sky. He sighed heavily. She jumped. "Is something wrong?"

"Nothing." His voice was unaccountably scratchy so instead of answering further he slumped deep into the seat and scowled until they reached Johns Falls and the commercial kitchen beside Carolyn Keen's house.

Carolyn had been busy. She had paperwork for all the necessary licenses to conduct a business in Minnesota in her hands because she was doing everything possible to expedite the process. Bruce said sotto voice, "She loves you or else she's very eager to be done with this place."

Carolyn's next words confirmed the rightness of his statements. "I tried to sell this building. I had it for sale for a year but no one was interested so I took it off the market." She stopped long enough to inspect the two people in front of her. "Just saying. If you are interested in the equipment or the whole works, building included, we can make a deal."

Abby gulped. "I'll have to see how things go." Everything was moving too fast for her to think straight and a look towards Bruce showed that he understood. He nodded just enough to give her courage a boost and she was grateful because she needed it.

Carolyn shooed them into the kitchen. "I think the place can be clean and functional by this afternoon if you want to get going on Mickey's first order."

Abby gulped again as the enormity of what she was undertaking hit her stomach and almost doubled her over. "I need a few things first. More muffin tins and such."

Carolyn nodded sagely. "Of course. Whatever I can do to help, just let me know." She disappeared after glancing around the kitchen and dancing happily across the floor. "I'm an expert, you know, and want to help you succeed."

When the door closed behind her, Bruce sniffed. "I told you she couldn't wait to retire." With which they found hot water and cleaned the place until it gleamed.

Becky then bought more muffin tins and enough ingredients to keep her busy for a month. "Except the strawberries are in the freezer at home because I didn't expect to get going so quickly."

"What say we grab lunch at Jerry's and then return home and get the berries? He has great pizza and wonderful cappuccino." He watched for her reaction.

She groaned in anticipation. "You have no idea how much I love cappuccino." So he was right. She had grown up with every convenience known to mankind, including a cappuccino machine or, at the very least, a nearby Starbucks where she undoubtedly spent many leisure hours while other, less fortunate people, toiled at menial jobs.

Jerry's was busy but they found a table near the front between two business owners on one side and an elderly couple treating their grandkids to pizza on the other. Soon both groups, along with everyone else in the place knew about Abby's new venture, thanks to Bruce's gift of gab, and more advice was sent her way than she'd ever be able to follow even if she knew what they were talking about, which she didn't. But she did recognize the friendship that was being offered along with the advice and smiled and smiled and smiled through the whole meal and several cappuccinos afterwards.

Rita Danforth and her grandkids promised to come to the next farmers' market because they loved home-made muffins, while Randy Wiles and Josiah Axos wanted to know if they could pick up muffins at the commercial kitchen on their way to open their stores in the morning because word had gotten around that Abby's muffins were to die for. "For breakfast and for pure enjoyment."

Glancing at Abby's expression and realizing that she didn't have a clue how to answer all those comments, Bruce assured everyone that they could easily get all the muffins they wanted once the business was up and running, which would be in a day or so and that, yes, Abby did know how to bake the best muffins on the planet.

When they left Jerry's, the day shone brighter than when they'd entered as Bruce turned Abby towards his truck. "I think you'll do a good muffin business."

"All I wanted was a cappuccino but I was mobbed, thanks to you."

"Publicity. You should learn how to publicize your business and, yes, you're the owner of a business and people are interested." He looked around at the small town that was in the process of awakening from a winter's nap and entering the busy summer season of long days and throngs of people on the streets.

"What if I fail? The whole town will laugh and no one will hire a failure."

"You'll do fine."

Abby tried to take everything in and failed completely. All she saw was muffins. And more muffins. And still more muffins. "I just want to sell enough to keep me going until I can get a job."

Bruce opened his mouth to reply, then shut it hard because she wouldn't hear what he was thinking. How good she was, how truly excellent her culinary creations were. That she had a business that would outshine any job available.

He peered down the street that already held a few vacationers, several farmers running errands, and a couple resort owners scrambling to get their places up and running before the influx of tourists hit the town and pandemonium commenced. The sight made him smile because he loved this start to summer. Always had loved it.

He turned away so Abby wouldn't think he was laughing at her because he wasn't but it was a glorious day and he was enjoying himself even if he was merely a resource person and a helper and maybe, now that he thought about it, a mentor because Abby certainly needed one and would continue to need one until she got her bearings in the business world.

A mentor might advise Abby that the summer ahead wouldn't be what she expected. It would be -- different. He couldn't guess how she'd feel about muffins once she realized what running a business would involve. She might hate them. Might never eat one again. All he knew was that owning a business would change her in some fundamental way he couldn't imagine.

Would she still be lovely and colorful when she finally emerged as a finished business woman if she decided to stay in business? Or would she take one look at the world of business once she figured out how it worked and run and hide? Judging from the last hour, it could go either way though he hoped that one day he'd peer into those gentian eyes and see excitement and happiness when she realized that her dreams were coming true and that muffins were an excellent business model.

She was a nice persona and deserved a good life even if she did come from a privileged background. And she was a good neighbor. And, though it didn't really matter in deciding whether or not she should have a good life, she was pretty, with lovely blue eyes. Interesting. And, remembering the feel of her in his arms when they were between a mother bear and its cubs, he recalled how soft and warm and feminine she was and how she'd fit perfectly against him. As if they were made for each other and in his entire life that hadn't been true of anyone else, ever, and it was a bit scary.

They bumped along the driveway to her house for the frozen berries and back again to the kitchen to make the first official batch of muffins. When they were done, they gave a dozen to Carolyn Keen, who protested that she'd never eat that many. Later they learned that she'd distributed most of them among her neighbors, all of who wanted more as soon as possible and Bruce wondered how exclusive the contract with Mickey's was. Maybe Abby could sell her muffins to other eateries? To individuals?

When they delivered that first batch of muffins to Mickeys late that afternoon, they were told that Abby could sell her muffins anywhere she wanted as long as she didn't charge less than Mickey did, which was easy because Mickey was too savvy a businessman to undercharge anyone. He had the lushest, most elegant restaurant in the Johns Falls area and his prices reflected that fact.

Then Mickey asked if Bruce should be consulted about everything business-wise and Bruce made sure that Mickey knew he was just helping out until Abby got her footing in the business world. Mickey nodded that he understood but gave Abby and Bruce a shrewd glance as they left his place. He shook his head and wondered how blind some people could be, anyway, and how long it would take them to realize that their relationship was way beyond that of mentor and student and into something far more complex.

He wasn't sure what that relationship was, whether it was a business partnership or something else, something more elemental. But they were definitely a pair, it showed in the way they walked, not side by side as individuals did, but as two halves of a whole.

He enjoyed people watching, it was one of the reasons he owned a restaurant, because there were so many interesting people to watch, and, as Bruce and Abby disappeared to wherever they were going, he decided that the summer ahead would be interesting.

CHAPTER 9

When Bruce and Abby finally got home, Abby offered him coffee. Or tea, she wasn't sure which, but it turned out he was happy with whatever was available so as the sun sank into the trees they gulped warmed-over coffee from the morning and didn't talk because they were too tired and too full of thoughts to speak.

Until Bruce turned to Abby and gazed at her for a long time. He wished he'd noticed before just how tired she was. Her new life was a difficult adjustment and it showed. "Your eyes have shadows. You're working too hard. You mustn't do that. You'll end up hating what you do."

She inspected him through half-lidded eyes. "You're the person who sent me to the farmers' market and I've been telling myself ever since that overwork must be part of being in business and I seem to be a business woman until I get a real job." At the moment, the fewer hours required by a job seemed more like a vacation than work.

Bruce slid deep into the cushy lounge and swirled coffee before swallowing. He considered how today had been a watershed day for Abby even if she didn't realize it because she was still focused on finding a normal, full-time job, a difficult task in the wilderness. But if she'd just recognize that she had a business of her own? The possibilities were endless.

Instead of looking for a job, she should be learning how to run the business that had fallen into her lap that would enable her to make a living in this beautiful place but she clearly wasn't ready to see that. So he decided to forgo trying to make her realize her good fortune. Instead, he spoke to her tiredness and said what he knew to be true because she'd not last long if she didn't rest once in a while. "Plan recreation into your schedule. Don't come to hate what you're doing."

With which he drank in both his coffee and the landscape that was turning a dozen shades of red and purple as the sun fell slowly into the trees and the way the setting sun glazed her hair gold. "Go swimming. Boating. Fishing. Something. Anything."

He stopped when he noticed with a tiny shock that there was no boat at her dock. Everyone living on a lake had a boat except him and he intended to own one as soon as possible. "Okay, there's not boat but you can swim off the dock until maybe someday you'll get a boat."

"I have a boat."

"You do?" His eyes were owl's eyes, large and black with surprise as he failed to find the boat she mentioned which was odd because the first thing everyone did when they arrived at a lake was to drag out a boat. Everyone except Abby, evidently.

She pointed. "There's one in the shed along the shore. An aluminum fishing boat with an outboard motor, if it still works." She couldn't remember when she and her grandmother had used them last.

She, too, slipped low in her lounge and watched the colors just as she and her grandmother had done many times over the years and a lump in her throat made speech impossible for a while, but after a while she was able to speak over it. "I do like to fish." Her grandmother had taught her. "If the motor works."

"Let's find out."

The small boat was in the boat house behind creaky doors. Bruce checked the outboard motor, yanking the starter rope until it roared to life. "Still works."

He dropped the rope and closed the door as the hinges protested loudly. "You have a working fishing boat." He was in awe of this fruit of her family's wealth that he'd have given a lot for as a child and still envied somewhat but that Abby hadn't seemed to remember until he mentioned it.

Just then, though, as they closed the door to the boathouse, mosquitoes arrived in clouds and they made a dash for the house, brushing the tiny bugs off of each other before entering so as not to let too many inside where they made a fresh pot of coffee and Abby found some cookies from her foray into town and said, in a sudden and complete about-face, "Let's do it. What you said. Take a break. Go fishing." Then she added," Both of us." Because Bruce probably knew more techniques than she did and he definitely knew what he was talking about when it came to business so she'd best do what he suggested. Take it easy. Take a day of rest.

"Tomorrow. Early."

He agreed and they watched the colors fade and the stars come out one by one to shine through the haze of mosquitoes until eventually the cloud of bugs thinned and then disappeared as always happened eventually and the night was clear once more. He put his cup in the sink and looked down at her. "I should go and, by the way, those cookies from the store weren't nearly as good as what you'll make when you add cookies to your list of baked goods to be sold in Johns Falls."

"Cookies?" She backed away to see him better and know if he was joking but she couldn't tell so she merely considered him, unable to think up a decent reply to such a ridiculous idea. "Cookies? Really?"

He tipped his head until they were inches apart, and said simply, "See you tomorrow."

Then he was gone in a bit more of a hurry than good manners required and she shut the door firmly behind him and told London that it was time for bed, with which the huge mongrel wagged his tail so hard that his whole body wagged in accompaniment and then he made a mad dash for the bed so he could get the best spot. As she crawled in after him and found enough space for herself around his huge body, she wondered if the three large dogs normally went fishing with their master. If so, how would they all fit in the boat?

When Bruce arrived the next morning, the boat was bobbing at the dock, Grandma Maude's tackle box was in it, the dogs seemed content to run around on the shore, and Abby was sitting on the dock examining the line on a pole. She looked up as he approached. "It's probably rotten but it's all I have and I'm not about to brave that driveway and go all the way to Johns Falls for more."

He joined her, yanked on the line, and they watched it disintegrate. "We can take turns with mine." He, too, had a tackle box and pole, plus a net and some nightcrawlers and probably knew as many ways to cook a shore lunch as her grandmother did.

When they returned, their stringer held enough panfish for one small meal and catching them had taken so many hours that the sun had already traversed two thirds of its daily route.

A quick, hot fire in the ring on the beach quickly turned to coals and they made short work of the fillets that Abby said were better than any she remembered. Or were the same but seemed better because it had been such a long time since she'd had a shore lunch. And, yes, Bruce was right that everyone needed time to relax and when she got around to it she'd tell him so.

Then they both fell asleep on the sand and, when they awoke, Bruce rose. Then, as she watched in semi-horror, he began stripping. Right before her eyes. Shoes first, kicked aside, and socks, then his shirt, then, as she didn't know whether to run into the house or stick around and enjoy the show, his belt buckle came off and he shimmied out of his jeans. And stood buck naked except for a faded but still serviceable pair of swimming trunks.

"Ready for a swim?"

She didn't know whether to laugh or cry. "As soon as I change." She ran into the house and slid into a one-piece suit that had cost a fortune and would soon lose its designer chic as the lake water faded it to much the same non-color as Bruce's trunks. Then she returned and they simply walked into the lake until their feet no longer touched bottom and then they swam.

When they emerged, Abby didn't know where the day had gone. "An entire day of doing nothing."

"Which was much needed." Bruce clapped a hand on her wet shoulder that was already drying in the sun and wind and this time she expected the electricity that came with his touch and looked for it and devoured it greedily. "Because soon you'll be so busy that you won't know whether you're a person or a machine and you'll wish you were a machine because they don't need sleep."

"If things go the way I hope, I'll soon inform Carolyn Keen that I no longer need her kitchen and I'll tell Mickey's that I can't provide him with any more muffins because I'll have a job. A real job, with a paycheck and benefits." She let her nose tilt up a bit and stepped daintily towards the house. "And enough time off to enjoy life. Like today."

Bruce followed silently while smiling broadly at this evidence of more spirit than he'd thought Abby possessed. And, as the thought crossed his mind, a second one followed. That it didn't matter. She was a nice, lovely woman whether she had spunk or not and that was all that was important. Life and, eventually, love, would find her, it always did, and he had the feeling that when it happened it would shape her into something special.

Love. Odd that the word came to him at that moment and God only knew why he was so interested in Abby Carr.

Come to think of it, God only knew why he was so invested in helping her become the owner of the house next door and God wasn't talking. He didn't have to be so helpful. He could easily back off and let her learn things on her own.

But he *was* invested in seeing that she succeeded and he *did* care and he didn't try to deny it and no matter what happened, he decided he'd keep it up. He'd do what he could to help this clueless woman earn the title to the property she loved, and along the way, teach her a few things about living in the wilderness as opposed to visiting it as she'd done as a child and he was inordinately glad that he had the necessary skills and knowledge.

"Want dinner?"

He looked at the fire ring on the beach, still glowing with coals that could cook steaks as well as fish. "Sure, and once the mosquitoes have buzzed their best for a couple hours, the rest of the evening will belong to us." He wanted to laugh because anyone listening would think they were lovers in some overly schmaltzy romance movie complete with a beach scene and over-hyped emotions instead of neighbors and quasi-business partners.

They spent the mosquito hours inside and, before the pesky critters disappeared, they got hungry so they made dinner on the six-burner stove and waved forks-full of steak at the hungry critters through the safety of the sliding glass doors. Bruce hated mosquitoes. "Worse than bears, actually. You can hide from bears."

"Both mosquitoes and bears eat people, just in different sized bites."

"I laugh at both from the safety of a sturdy house with screens on all the windows."

As the last glow of day disappeared and the deep dark that can only be experienced in a forest at night settled over them, they turned out the lights and went outside to watch the stars. Bruce pointed. "It's what I do for recreation. Watch day and night begin and end. Make sure the stars stay where they belong. Check if the moon is still on duty. And, occasionally spot a satellite to remind me that I'm not living in the past."

Abby shivered slightly and Bruce moved unconsciously closer. She thought the move was unconscious, that he didn't know what he was doing. Then her thoughts changed course and she wondered if he did know and unaccountably hoped that was the case. She willed the shivering to stop without him touching her and then she started counting stars until he asked, "You plan on counting all night?"

She smiled in the dark, suddenly realizing that she was totally comfortable with this next-door neighbor as neighbors are counted in the forest, bulging muscles, helpful suggestions, electric touches, and all. "You can't see stars from the forest. Just in this small clearing by the lake. So I count them when I can."

With her face raised, she couldn't see him move still closer but she felt it. Heard his breathing mix with the breeze. Felt his bulk loom near. Saw his face in memory. Wondered if his eyes were as dark as that first day when they faced down a bear or the other times she'd seen into their darkness. Or were they lighter? Laughing? Were his arms as hard as the steel they'd felt like as he held her safe, though she knew it had been her imagination coupled with a desperate desire to stay alive. His whole body had seemed hard enough that any bear tearing into him would break its teeth.

Pity the poor bear. Picturing its broken teeth, she giggled.

He looked down at her upturned face. "Stars are funny?"

"Not stars. Bears."

A moment of silence, then, "Okay. We're going from stars to bears." He smiled too, in the dark, she could feel it, hear it in his next words. "I'm not going to ask where the change in topic came from because I suspect the answer would take an hour or so."

She giggled again and he reached up as if to pluck a star and give it to her and she knew that he was glad for the day, for the invitation to dinner, for the stars and the night sky and even for her at his side. She didn't know how she knew all those things, but she did and the knowing made her warm and happy.

But it was time for him to leave because tomorrow would be a busy day and he looked at her, wondering if she knew how busy her life could become if her muffin business took off the way he suspected it would. When he'd first met Carolyn Keen, she'd described being similarly surprised when she started selling pies and learned people actually would pay money for them. The remembrance of that conversation had been the impetus for him to suggest Abby sell muffins and he was proud of giving her a shove into business ownership.

But now, tonight, it was time for him to step back and give her time to think. To plan. To figure out her next step. If she asked for help, of course he'd stick around for a bit longer than he planned to. He'd do whatever he could to help her get her feet wet in the world of business.

Not that the sticking around would be for any reason other than being a helpful neighbor because what other reason could there be?

CHAPTER 10

Abby took a deep breath, unlocked the commercial kitchen's door and stepped inside. She was alone so it took courage because today would be the first day she'd be baking, cooling, wrapping and delivering muffins on her own. And, oh yes, there'd be cupcakes from Grandma Maude's recipes as well as muffins so she'd best get busy.

She turned on the oven to pre-heat and pulled the huge mixer close and got busy and soon she'd forgotten her original trepidation in the details – and the enjoyment – of muffins and cupcakes. And soon, she decided, remembering Bruce's suggestion, there'd be cookies. Because she liked cookies and was fairly sure her grandmother had recipes for those, too.

Carolyn dropped in to see how she was doing, glance around the kitchen and make sure everything was being done right, and said she'd be at home if Abby needed anything. Asked if Abby had her kitchen manager's license yet. Then she left and Abby went back to her baking.

Until the door opened again. "What is it, Carolyn?"

"Who's Carolyn?" A familiar voice met her ears.

Abby swung around. "Denise!" She gave her friend a

hug. "What brings you to Johns Falls? And how'd you know where to find me?"

Denise stepped into the kitchen and looked around with something approaching awe as she explained that she was with her family at a nearby resort for an early summer weekend and when she'd gone to the house in the forest to find Abby, it had been empty but she'd met a really hot guy on the way out who told her where to find her friend. "Wow! He's gorgeous and he's unattached – I asked -- and he's your next-door neighbor! How cool is that?"

"We are just friends." The timer went off and Abby took out three trays of muffins and put them on the cooling racks. "Yes, he's nice but if you want to go after him, you have my blessings." Then she thought. "But I doubt if it will do much good because I think he's the bachelor type."

"You think he's not into you or you think he's not into anyone?" Denise examined her friend and sniffed. "If that's what you're thinking, then you're wrong because he is interested in you. In Abby Carr. In fact, I think he's very interested judging by how much he talked about you." She thought back on her earlier conversation with Bruce. "And also judging by his tone of voice and how much he said. He rambled on and on about you. And then there was the look on his face every time he said your name."

Abby flushed and mumbled, "I have to get these muffins done pronto," and pretended the heat from the ovens was the reason her face was red. Because Bruce wasn't into her. Couldn't be. She'd know if he was. Wouldn't she?

Denise continued her curious inspection of the kitchen. "So how exactly does this muffin thing work? Your neighbor who you say is not interested in you when he absolutely is more than interested said that you're selling muffins and other stuff to a restaurant in town." She shook her head. "I'd never have expected to see my childhood friend and confidante, Abby Carr, bake muffins for a living."

"It's not for a living. It's temporary and I should be

getting more muffins out of their tins." She turned from Denise as the timer went off again and proceeded to turn the muffins that were barely cool enough to touch out of their tins and managed to take a long time because the blushing refused to stop. Darn it anyway and had Denise always been so perceptive? Yes, she had.

Denise stepped gingerly further into the kitchen. "You look busy."

"I am." Fussing with muffins and cooling racks and hiding from her childhood friend's perceptive visit.

"Is there anything I can do to help?" Looking about and hoping the answer would be negative.

"I don't think so, but thanks for the offer." Still facing away from Denise until the red faded, at least enough that the heat from the ovens would account for it. "And thanks for stopping by."

Denise looked about again, finally figuring out how things worked. The ovens, the cooling racks, the table for wrapping. "If I can't help then I suspect the best thing I can do is disappear because you seem to be very busy." She moved backwards towards the door.

Abby flushed again, this time from embarrassment at treating one of her best friends shoddily. "I didn't mean to be rude."

"You're not rude. Just busy." Trust Denise to be nice.

Abby flushed still more but after Denise left she admitted privately that she was glad. They were friends, had been since they were small, but today that friendship had to take a back seat to muffins. Even if the muffin business was temporary. Which it was, no doubt about that.

Then she forgot Denise in the rush of making muffins and deciding how many cupcakes to make for Mickeys and the farmers' market on Saturday.

When Saturday arrived, she didn't attend the farmers' market after all. Bruce said he'd sell her wares for her so she could work in the kitchen, an offer she gratefully accepted.

Late Saturday afternoon, after the market closed, he stopped by the kitchen. Gave Abby the money he'd collected for her wares and told her that he could have sold more if there'd been more to sell. "Word is getting around and people are coming specifically for your muffins." But he refused to accept payment for helping, saying he was there anyway and that it was fun.

As they talked, there was a knock on the door, which was odd because no one knocked. They just walked in. Abby opened the door and found herself staring in shock at her parents. "Mom. Dad."

Her mother was her usual impeccable self in designer jeans and an elegant, light summer sweater with several strands of obviously real pearls around her neck and more dangling from her ears. Her father, who was by nature a bit more reserved, wore jogging shoes that cost more than most people made in a week and, like everything else he wore, came from LL Bean because they were in the north woods and that's what people he knew wore in the great out-of-doors.

Bruce took one look at them, glanced at his own tough but hard-used work clothes, and went very still. Moved a couple steps backwards. Put a table between Abby's parents and himself. Twitched and fidgeted until he realized what he was doing and made himself go still and listen politely to the elder Carrs.

Her mother spoke first, casting a curious sidewise glance at Bruce. "We came for a visit, dear, and came straight to the kitchen instead of the house in the forest because this is where Denise had said you'd be. Said you're probably here most of the time." Her frown said that wasn't a good thing.

"You spoke with Denise?" What on earth had Denise said to her parents that had sent them rocketing to Johns Falls? No matter what pretend reason they were using for their visit, they were here to check on her. Did Denise tell them that Abby was drowning in muffins? Too busy to visit with a friend? Or did she describe Abby's hot next-door neighbor and they had to see what was going on in the romance department?

Both parents wore concerned expressions and had all kinds of excuses for coming right then. Too many excuses. "Summer is just around the corner. Thought we'd get a jump on the tourists and come now." Which meant that whatever Denise said had truly had them concerned.

Bruce wasn't dumb. He knew the senior Carrs were checking on their daughter and he knew that he could be part of the inspection. No wonder he skulked behind a counter of muffins.

Abby's father looked around the kitchen, missing nothing, especially not Bruce. The elder Carr's gaze met Bruce's but neither man spoke as Abby's father asked, "Got room for us at the house, Abby, or should we rent a room somewhere?"

"Of course she has room and who is this gentleman?" Her mother examined Bruce while pretending to examine muffins. So, yes, this visit was about Bruce even though her mother said smoothly, "Denise said you work too hard." She looked her daughter up and down while managing to examine Bruce at the same time. "She was right. You are exhausted."

Bruce sidled towards the door, muttering something about feeding the dogs, after which he disappeared in a cloud of dust as Abby's parents watched in pretend surprise and her mother asked innocently, "Is that the next-door neighbor Denise mentioned?"

Abby groaned and nodded. "Bruce Merriweather." She dug deep for an excuse for Bruce's quick departure. "He's a very considerate person. He's giving us time to ourselves."

In a surprisingly short time, the Carr family ended up at the house in the forest thanks to Abby's parents helping make muffins so everything was done in double time and there were enough for Mickey's restaurant even after selling out at the farmers' market and her mother didn't care that her expensive clothes were white with flour because she'd been helping her daughter.

Her mother nibbled a muffin delicately, before giving the rest of the muffin to her father. "I'd forgotten how good your mother's muffins are, Ed."

"Mom's great in a bakery. Could have been a professional."

"Looks like Abby is the professional your mother could have been. A nice tribute to her."

They dropped into chairs on the deck like everyone who'd ever visited, and Abby brought them pop and some cupcakes she'd brought from the commercial kitchen because she didn't have anything at home for dessert and they made short work of both and then mentioned that perhaps they should have dinner, no matter that they'd already had dessert.

Her father brushed crumbs from his lap. "Reminds me of the good times we had here when I was a kid. Mom always had something special from the oven."

Her mother stretched and smiled in placid contentment. "And then you married me. Good thing you can cook."

Her father laughed and gave his wife an airy wave. "Yep. Good thing." He then turned to Abby and, as casually as possible, said, "Tell me about your neighbor. The guy at the kitchen who got out of there as if spooked and it was because there's something going on between you two and he was embarrassed and don't try to pretend otherwise"

Abby flushed. What to say? Something nice without making it look like the 'something' was more than it was. Then she knew the single best thing she could say that was positive and true and guaranteed to stop her parents' inquiries. "I met him my first day here. In the forest. He saved my life."

The elder Carrs sat up straight. "He what? Saved your

life? How?" So Abby related the incident with the mother bear and its cubs. "And that's why I have one of his dogs now." They'd seen London but hadn't gotten around yet to asking when Abby had acquired a dog. "Because that bear family is still in the woods and London, here, will tell me in time for me to leave the bear family alone. And if the bear decides to be pushy, London will keep it away from me."

The Carrs were silent for a long time. Then Abby's mother said slowly, fighting tears, "Can we meet your friend? Again? Truly meet him this time instead of' hello' and 'goodbye?' So we can thank him properly for saving our only child's life?"

It was a reasonable request. Abby immediately phoned Bruce and invited him for lunch after church on Sunday. He was reluctant but agreed when Abby explained why her parents wanted to meet him.

They nodded to him in church the next Sunday but he was already seated several pews ahead of them and afterwards he was lost in the throng of people having coffee and cookies and generally being sociable. But he did stop by Abby's house in the forest on his way home and sat awkwardly, politely, on a chair on the deck, staring hard at the sun's rays glinting off the lake, playing with London, ruffling his coat, whispering to him and being licked in return while generally avoiding the humans on the deck.

"Tell me about the bear incident." A direct request from Abby's father to Bruce couldn't very well be ignored so Bruce told him about going for strawberries and ending up pulling Abby out of the bear's path.

Abby's mother started to say 'thank you' but teared up and couldn't finish, finally waving to indicate that she couldn't speak. When she eventually calmed down, she simply said, "Thank you for saving our daughter's life."

"I doubt she was in any real danger."

Abby's father moved closer to Bruce and warily petted London because he was a very large dog and Ed Carr didn't know him but wanted to acknowledge what he'd done. "Your dog lives with our daughter now. That says there's still a bear family in the woods and as long as they are there, there's also potential danger."

Bruce raised his eyes to the elder Carr and silently acknowledged that the forest could be a place of danger. Both nodded briefly, each having lived in the forest at one time or another, then Bruce went back to petting London with Ed Carr watching. But he seemed more relaxed, less stressed, than before. Abby silently thanked her father for being the person he was. A man who understood other men.

Abby and her father made dinner while Bruce and Robin Carr stayed on the deck and talked. At least they tried to talk but Abby suspected their conversation consisted more of pat questions and answers than getting to know one another. Unlike her husband, Robin had grown up in the city and only knew about the wilderness from visits to this very house when her children were growing up and it contained every convenience known to mankind and was totally safe.

When the sun dropped precipitously behind the trees, Bruce took his leave and Abby and London walked him to his truck. He gave his dog one last hug. "It was nice meeting your parents."

"Liar. You hated every second of the visit and are glad it's over."

Bruce sagged. "They are – intimidating."

"Intimidating? My parents?" She couldn't believe what she was hearing. Her parents were the most laid-back people she knew.

"Maybe not your folks themselves. But their clothes. And their car--" He spared a look at the Carr's brand new SUV that could handle any terrain and had cost a fortune.

Money. Too much of it was in that SUV and that bothered Bruce, or at least more money than his family evidently had. But she couldn't tell him it was silly to feel that way because it wouldn't change anything. She thought hard what to say, finally settling on, "They grow on you. Given enough time, I'm sure you'll all become the best of friends."

A low growl in Bruce's throat said what odds he gave of that ever happening, then he hopped into his truck, pulled carefully around the Carr's subtle blue SUV and left, with Abby staring after him wondering if she had it in her to become a bridge between her helpful neighbor and her beloved parents.

She willingly accepted the responsibility because she liked Bruce and loved her parents and they both were important to her, though why Bruce, who was just a neighbor, was equal in importance to her parents she couldn't fathom. Maybe because he saved her life? Watching the dust settle on the driveway before turning back to her parents, she decided that was probably it.

And when she went to bed that night after staying up many hours later than usual talking with her parents, she fell asleep remembering Bruce's throaty growl. Did he know how sexy it was?

CHAPTER 11

Abby's parents stayed for a few days of helping make muffins and then left with promises to come again and pleas for her not to work too hard. They asked her to say 'good-by' to Bruce for them. She did as requested and soon settled into a routine of working weekdays at the kitchen in Johns Falls, getting ingredients on Monday, baking on Tuesday, Wednesday, and Thursday, and delivering baked goods on Friday. It worked. Until school let out for the summer and the real vacation season started.

Just as the first vacationers arrived, she got her kitchen manager's license and told Carolyn she was no longer needed and thanked her for her help. Sending her away was probably a mistake because it meant she lost the small bit of help that she'd got from the previous owner of the bakery. As it turned out, she could have used that help because suddenly she was swamped.

So she put in longer hours at the kitchen, arriving at the crack of dawn and leaving at dark which was close to the middle of the night in this land of long summer evenings.

She stopped selling at the farmers' market because she didn't have enough muffins or anything else left after supplying Mickey's Pub and the two other restaurants in the area that had come looking for her baked goods. At the time she'd been glad for the business. Now she wasn't so sure but the money was much appreciated until she got a real job. So she worked hard to satisfy everyone.

The money was surprisingly good. Not that it would last, of course, because sales were high only because the summer tourist season was in full swing and the streets of Johns Falls were thronged with visitors and summer residents. But they were temporary people. When school started again in the autumn and the snow began to fall, those streets would be close to empty and many of the stores would close for the winter.

Until then she was happy for this unexpected financial bonus. Each evening, when closing the kitchen and heading home, she found herself tired but happy, surprised at how much she enjoyed baking. The wonderful smells. The satisfaction of seeing her creations unfold.

Soon, as she'd said would happen, she added cookies to her repertoire after calling Grandma Maude for ideas because her grandmother's recipes seemed to be what people wanted. Her grandmother emailed them without hesitation and mentioned that Abby seemed to be settling into her new life nicely. Her voice, from the sunny shores of the Caribbean, was warm and happy.

Abby didn't see Bruce – didn't have time to see

him – until one Wednesday afternoon – his usual day to go to town and do necessary shopping -- when he stopped by the kitchen to see how she was doing. What she was doing. Why she'd disappeared from his life. He found her deep in muffin batter and cookie recipes with shadows under her eyes and hair that hadn't seen a beauty shop in ages and was tied severely back.

He looked around, seeing everything. How busy she was. How overworked. "Need some help?"

She blew an errant strand of hair away. "If you have the time." Carefully worded because he had a life, too. He spent many hours selling lovely pictures on birch bark and even more painting them and doing medical billing. He was probably as tired as she was. But, my oh my, could she ever use some help!

His answer was to wash his hands and find one of the huge aprons that came with the kitchen. "Tell me what to do." He looked around at the racks of muffins and cupcakes and cookies. Sniffed the aromatic air. Smiled. "Looks like you are doing a booming business." Stood a bit taller and puffed out his chest a bit. "This was a good idea of mine. Glad I pointed you in the direction of a muffin business."

"It's temporary," she replied automatically as she'd said to her parents and anyone else who asked and wasn't a customer, wondering how come this small indication of his pride didn't bother her, rather made her smile. "Come winter, customers will disappear and leave me without an income. So I still need to find a job." And how she'd find the time to visit all the businesses in Johns Falls to remind them that she was available was more than she could figure. "When things slow down enough for me to put in applications."

"Hmmm," was his laconic reply as he measured flour and sugar into a huge bowl and pulled strawberries from the freezer.

She looked to see if he was joking but he was deep in flour and sugar so she couldn't see his expression. What she did see was the way his muscles flexed handling the huge flour and sugar bins as if they were feathers. She didn't even try, using a scoop to avoid lifting the heavy containers. And the way he tilted his head, not enough for her to see his eyes, just enough to make sure his aim was true so he didn't spill flour all over everything as he weighed it carefully.

Dark eyes, as she recalled, and expressive, at least they had been when she'd almost been eaten by a bear. And every other time she'd had occasion to peer into them. Dark enough to remember clearly, fringed by straight lashes and with a perpetual squint from being outdoors. There were tiny creases at the corners, undoubtedly from wind and sun.

And what was she doing obsessing about a man's eyes, anyway, when there was work to be done? Muffins to be baked. Cookie dough to be scooped onto sheets. And at the end of the week, deliveries to be made and checks to be collected.

"Is something wrong?" She could see his eyes now, in a frowning face as he looked downward to see if there was flour on his jeans or some similar reason behind her stare. She colored, said things were fine, and turned away. Hoped he accepted her lame explanation. Figured he knew exactly what she'd been thinking. Swore to keep her mind on her work and couldn't because all she could think about was the way his jeans fit, the ones without any flour on them yet but would soon because he was deep in flour and sugar. After many washings and hard use, they were molded to legs as muscular as the arms that lifted heavy containers so easily. Drat!

"What do you call your business, anyway?" His question brought her back to reality. "Got a name for it?"

"I never thought about it."

"Names are good. People remember better where their favorite muffins come from if there's a name."

"This whole thing is temporary." So there was no need for a name.

Bruce stopped what he was doing. Turned. Leaned back against a counter and considered her with a small shake of his head. "You do know that you have a viable business here, don't you? One with the potential to support you year around?"

Abby laughed. "Winter will come and when it does, this business will disappear. By the time snow arrives, customers will be gone."

Bruce shook his head again and muttered something about block-headed women, but he returned to his flour and sugar, which by then was in one of the two commercial mixers on one side of the kitchen, along with butter and eggs and other interesting ingredients. The huge mixers that Abby could barely control while tipping dough from them and into muffin tins. The same mixers that Bruce manipulated easily with one hand.

As she regarded him humming happily as he worked, Abby couldn't decide whether to be depressed because she'd never match his physical prowess or happy because she had a nice, if temporary, income that might eventually lead to owning the house in the forest and she also had a friend who seemed to show up at the most propitious times.

She paused in her work and watched him for a moment. The rhythm of his movements, the strength that spoke of a lifetime of physical labor, the dark eyes that, at the moment, were pools of contentment. "You enjoy baking, don't you, Bruce?"

He stopped long enough to look up and grin. "I always liked helping my mom. Living back to nature she baked all our bread and everything else." He sniffed the air. "As a kid, I thought the smell was heaven." Waved a hand. "Like this place." He took a deep breath and closed his eyes in ecstasy and Abby found herself doing the same and, yes, it was wonderful and evocative and strangely, inexplicably, unsettling though she couldn't know whether that was because of the heavenly smells or the man across the room.

CHAPTER 12

Bruce stopped by every so often during the coming weeks. He knew how busy a tourist town like Johns Falls could get during the summer season because he depended on that very thing to sell his pictures. And, as he explained each and every time he came, he enjoyed baking. Enjoyed having muffins for lunch and never grew tired of them because there were so many different fillings that he never repeated once in a week's worth of nibbling.

Many days he was the only one baking muffins and cupcakes because Abby was busy in the somewhat small office on one side of the commercial kitchen where she went over receipts and inventory and more kinds of paperwork than she'd have believed possible.

She had a tiny muffin business, not a huge international corporation, but there were times when she wasn't sure there was much difference as far as paperwork was concerned. On such days – and there were more than she'd have believed possible – she was glad for Bruce's help and secretly concerned that one day he'd inform her that he no longer had the time to spend on muffins and other miscellaneous baked goods. That he had an actual life to live.

She'd be in a world of hurt if that happened, not to mention that she'd miss his company. She finally decided to stop worrying herself to death over the possibility and gathered up her courage and asked Bruce if he'd be okay with coming in on a schedule she could depend on.

His reply was evasive. "I realize that this whole business seems overwhelming now but once you get the hang of things it'll be easier and you'll get all that paperwork done in no time. Then you'll have more time to spend on the actual business of muffins."

She didn't believe him because she was learning what was involved and it was a lot. So she remained in panic mode. "Please, Bruce, don't quit on me. And if you must stop helping, please let me know before you stop coming so I can prepare." She hated admitting how much she needed him but it was the simple truth. "Give me warning because I'll need it. A lot of warning. A whole lot."

His eyebrows rose. "Really? You're that snowed under?" He looked around in surprise. The kitchen was clean and well-organized, but that could be because Abby was better at the business thing than he'd expected of a pampered only child.

She nodded. "I am overwhelmed and getting more so all the time. In fact –" She stopped suddenly as her eyes opened wide and her face lit up because an idea had come to her. A brainstorm. An epiphany. "In fact, if you'll agree to work here formally – like in being an employee who shows up regularly– I'll be happy to pay you a percentage like I'm paying Carolyn for use of the kitchen." She nibbled her lower lip. "I think I can afford you. I'll have to check my figures but, thanks to all those hours spent pouring over paperwork, I'm pretty sure I know where I stand financially and that I'm in a good enough place to afford an employee."

He frowned and her heart sank. "I'm not sure I have the time. The medical billing is picking up and after getting the generator going and filling it with fuel and making room on the kitchen table and everything else I must do before even getting started on the actual billing, the whole endeavor takes more time than you'd think. I make very little per hour because I don't have power full time and I both live and work in a small place." He scratched the back of his head as his frown deepened. "Though I'd love to work for you on a regular basis if I could, and not because of the money, either. It's fun. And I love muffins."

He scratched his head a second time and continued. "Okay, I admit it. I'm here today because I suspected you were strapped and might need an extra hand and I can do one thing for you. I promise not to leave today until you're caught up or we both drop of exhaustion. But I also am here today and every time I come because I like baking muffins. With you.

"Okay, I'll make one more promise." He held up a hand in a swearing motion. "I'll come as often as possible given my work schedule at home and I'll continue to take my pay in muffins." He paused, seeing her unhappy expression. "That might not be as much as you want but it's all I'm comfortable promising."

It was the best she could get and Abby chose to be grateful for the hours they worked side by side, mixing, filling, baking, wrapping and labeling muffins, cupcakes and cookies, so she said no more about hiring him. Bruce was a conscientious worker who sang softly as he moved about the kitchen. Opera, which made Abby smile. She recognized Wagner's 'Ring' music.

She could picture his childhood home with no electricity but probably a wind-up phonograph or battery-operated radio and college-educated parents who were making sure their only child got a proper education and, hence, supervised what music he heard. Former professors who liked opera. With limited input from the outside world he probably hadn't heard rock or hip-hop until he was an adult.

Thinking about him, she found herself staring at him. He noticed. Colored. Switched from Wagner to a Sousa march and Abby knew she was right and that his musical education had included marches as well as opera. And why that knowledge warmed her inside and out she didn't know except that it made this former military type and all-around competent woodsman more human.

After that, they worked for a while in a silence broken only by Bruce's occasional low humming. Wagner and Sousa, punctuated by *West Side Story*. Until they both reached for the huge cannister of flour that held more pounds than Abby'd thought one container could hold before she became a tiny part of the commercial food industry. Now, of course, she knew better. They were huge and held a lot of flour. A whole lot.

Anyway, their hands and arms somehow met and, possibly because of that electricity that happened every time they touched, they bumbled together until the cannister went over. And landed sidewise on the floor and bounced a couple of times and then rolled until all the flour spilled out in a white pile that slid across the room like a sand dune in motion as some of it drifted up into the air in a white, bright cloud that blocked the sun coming in the window.

They stared at the ever-expanding whiteness in horror. Then at each other. They were as white as ghosts.

The humor of the situation hit them both at the same time. The way they looked, the white cloud that was slowly but surely engulfing the room. And, quietly at first but with an ever-growing sense of the humor of the situation they began to laugh, louder and then louder, holding sleeves to their faces so as not to breathe in flour dust while trying to keep their mouths closed so as not to ingest the white stuff even though it was impossible because they were laughing and laughing involved opened mouths.

They kept laughing and sitting in flour until they ended up covered in white – white clothes, white hair, white eyebrows -- and that, too, seemed suddenly funny and they almost rolled on the floor in hilarity, except, if they had actually rolled, they'd have been even whiter so, instead, they wrapped their arms around each other and held on tight to keep themselves off the floor and out of the ever-spreading cloud.

At which moment, the door opened and the owner of the candy store in town stepped inside. Saw them. Blinked. Smiled tentatively and took a second step, carefully avoiding a drift of white that had somehow managed to fly all the way across the room until it reached the door. Examined their entwined selves. Flushed and looked every which way except directly at them. And asked, "Did I come at a bad time?"

Abby groaned. Moaned. Spit out a few mouthfuls of flour. Looked to Bruce for help and found him to be no help at all because he was laughing while the newcomer waited to see what she'd say. What she'd do. How she'd explain a kitchen filled with flour everywhere except where it was supposed to be with two entwined people rolling in the stuff.

She gave up. Lifted her hands and blew on them, then watched the flour fly through the air. "Depends." The candy store owner still waited. "On whether you can see the humor of a room full of flour or whether you are here for a more serious purpose." She examined him again, more closely. "What do you want, anyway?" Recognized him. "You're the candy man, aren't you?"

He half bowed. "At your service and I'm interested in carrying your cookies as an addition to my candy." He looked around again, slowly this time, as a tiny smile started at one corner of his mouth and grew until his face twitched with the effort not to laugh. "And, yes, this place is funny at the moment. But I'm truly interested in cookies if you have any available after this --" He searched for a word. "-- flour debacle is remedied."

"Remedied." Abby considered the word. "If by 'remedied,' you mean vacuumed, swept, mopped, and washed -- everything in the entire kitchen -- and then a repeat of the process a few times, yes I might be interested."

She remembered how busy she was and that Bruce's help couldn't be depended on. So she hedged. Groaned. "I mean that I truly am interested and when this is cleaned up, maybe we can talk." She looked woefully around the room. "But that could be a while because I have no idea how long it'll take to make this place normal again."

Her face fell, she couldn't help it, and couldn't help that the newcomer saw her despair. "A long while because the entire place will have to be cleaned and sanitized" She knew the rules and regulations on commercial kitchen cleanliness, having gotten her kitchen manager's license. "It'll be a huge undertaking."

With which her laughter died at the thought of the daunting task ahead. And the time it would take. And the fact that she'd not be able to work in the kitchen until it was completely sanitized and that might mean her customers would be left high and dry.

The newcomer thought a moment as if he knew what she was thinking, which he probably did because he, too, sold food and had to meet the same health standards she did. "I bet I know people who will help." He paused and his eyes lit up once again held-back laughter. "If you don't mind a few jokes at your expense when they arrive and see the mess."

Abby waved her arms to indicate the white kitchen. "We were laughing our heads off so I guess other people can too." She rose, followed by Bruce, then came close to the newcomer but didn't touch him because if she did, he'd turn white too. "Do you really think anyone will help? It's my mess. My fault. My responsibility."

"The entire town of Johns Falls is dying of curiosity about your business. The business people will jump at the chance to see what you're up to and it's pretty close to quitting time for those who don't stay open evenings and those that do have hired help because they'd rather die than spend all day and then all evening at work."

He backed towards the door. "I'll be back in a sec, and if I'm right, I'll bring a mop brigade because people who own businesses know how to clean because it's amazing how messy places can get during a normal business day. They have lots of experience." He looked around one last time before disappearing. "Though I will say that this flour debacle is over the top, even for Johns Falls."

Abby and Bruce meant to start cleaning instead of waiting for help but every time they moved even an inch, clouds of white flew around them and they started laughing again so not much was accomplished until the first contingent of business people arrived.

Jerry of Jerry's Pizza tiptoed delicately across the now-white floor and held out a hand, first to Abby and then to Bruce, after which he examined the white hand that had held theirs, as if saying that he wasn't afraid of ghosts.

Chloe from the Garden Center pressed her lips in a straight line to suppress laughter until she realized that laughter was acceptable and then she giggled as she brought a very large, heavy-duty outdoor vacuum -- normally used to suck leaves and other debris from the outdoor portion of the Garden Center – into the kitchen and began competently sucking up white stuff.

The candy store owner, who was organizing the

rescue effort, ducked in to deliver two more business owners and show the man from the elevator what needed doing.

All the help gave Abby the necessary impetus to swing into action herself and soon she was swabbing down counters and ovens and the rest of the kitchen equipment. She reached the door to the tiny office and stopped. Looked inside. Breathed a sigh of relief that, through some fortuitous circumstance, none of the white stuff had invaded the room, and slowly, carefully, in order not to disturb any of the flour that still remained and send it shooting into the office, she closed the door.

As she stared at the tiny office through the glass door, she had an idea, though it would have to wait to be fully vetted until the hoard of workers was gone and the place was once again pristine. An idea that, if Bruce agreed, would carry her business physically and financially through the busy summer months and into autumn when, hopefully, a job would open up and she could forget about muffins.

She did enjoy the work. Hadn't expected to like it quite as much as she did, but every time she slid a tray of muffins into one of the ovens, a picture of her grandmother and the times they'd spent at the house in the forest rose before her and that added another dimension to the simple enjoyment of baking.

Soon – way sooner than Abby would have thought possible given the extent of the white cloud that had settled over everything – the kitchen began to once again resemble a kitchen.

But no one left when the work was completed. Instead, Jerry provided pizzas and someone else found ice cream and Carolyn, who'd come from next door to see what the commotion was all about, made a couple tons of iced tea and everyone had a party.

They left the kitchen because they didn't want to get it dirty after having just spent so much time cleaning it. Instead, they adjourned to the outside and spread across the small, grassy space behind the building and from there on into Carolyn's yard and everyone found a tree trunk to lean against or a chair to sit in or a piece of grass to ease onto and they sat around and asked Abby a million questions about her business while chowing down on pizza and ice cream.

How'd she like being a business woman? What were her future plans? Was the muffin business going to be year-around or seasonal? What else did she plan to bake in the future? How'd she like working and living in Johns Falls?

She didn't know what to say. Didn't want to tell them this was just a temporary gig, not after they'd all worked so hard. So she hedged, not exactly lying but not telling the whole truth either.

She said that she hadn't firmed up her plans yet. That the business had been so unexpected and had gotten busy so fast that she hadn't had time to think about the future. To make decisions.

They nodded their collective heads as if her story was familiar. As if every business owner had gone through something similar and no one had intentionally started a business. As if all of them had fallen into business accidentally, though, of course, they couldn't have done so.

Surely her story was unique, unless all the businesses in town just happened and she doubted that very much until Jerry of Jerry's Pizza commented in a general sort of way that small town businesses were different than businesses in big cities. Less of a decision to go for a particular business and more of a life direction. Less button-down business ethic and more life-style. And then she wasn't so sure she was different after all.

Not that it mattered. When a decent job opened up, she'd close down the muffin business in a heartbeat and jump at the chance to work for someone else.

CHAPTER 13

The business owners left, one by one, saying how glad they were to finally meet the owner of the muffin business and that she was welcome and a true asset to Johns Falls. As she waved the last one off, she turned to Bruce because the idea that had sprung full-blown when she glanced into the office in the kitchen hadn't disappeared. Had been waiting for this moment.

Had grown until she was sure – absolutely positive – that it would work and solve both of their problems, at least until she got a job. Not only would it do that, after making a deal with the candy store owner to provide him with cookies, which was about to place an even heavier burden of time and work on her, it had better work or she'd be in a bad place.

She looked at Bruce and took a deep breath. He was flat on the grass gazing at the stars that were out because it had taken a long time to clean the kitchen and have a party afterwards. Night was in full swing. He took in the sweep of the sky with one arm. "I don't see stars much at home. Too many trees. I believe we talked about that once."

"I like trees so I'm okay with darkness."

"I do too but stars are nice once in a while." He patted the grass beside him. "Join me. Look up. See for yourself."

A shooting star whizzed through the firmament and disappeared. "A couple of miles away. Want to go look for it?"

Abby laughed. "You know perfectly well it burned up before reaching the ground."

"I do." He sounded lazy. Comfortable. "But it's nice to imagine there's a star out there somewhere in the forest just waiting to be found. All blue and glowing and warm and full of wishes to be granted to whomever finds it."

She lowered herself to the grass beside him. It was still warm from the heat of the day and felt good to her battered self. "Bruce, I want to talk. I have a proposition."

"Uh oh." Then, after a pause. "That sounds ominous. But perhaps it's to be expected because you are a new business owner and any business requires much thought." He waved at the sky again. "Even with all this beauty above us, you don't stop thinking about muffins and the other baked goods that seem to be wanted by everyone who samples them even once."

He rolled enough to look at her. They were inches apart. She could see his eyes shine in the dark, reflecting the stars and wispy night clouds, feel his breath, almost feel that something that she'd already figured out was unique to him. The electricity that came from touching him ever since the bear encounter but now she knew it was more than that. More than the bear incident. She thought of it as the Bruce effect for lack of any better explanation.

The first time she'd noticed it, of course, had been when he'd backed her away from the bear in the forest and so she'd thought of it as that, a safe, masculine surety that she'd be okay because he'd take care of her. But it had been there every time they'd been together since. An electricity she couldn't explain and had given up trying. It was just there, Bruce incarnate, and she couldn't push it away. Couldn't ignore it. And didn't want to.

So she didn't pull away now though discretion indicated she should. Instead she simply lay with her head pillowed on one arm and waited to see what he'd do. If anything. And when he'd do it. If ever.

He did. Slowly, ever so slowly, he moved closer. Then closer still. Until their lips met and she didn't pull away, didn't want to, enjoyed every moment of their togetherness, every sensation that coursed through her body, head to toes. Closed her eyes to savor him better. Wondered why this particular man was so much more enjoyable than any others she'd kissed in similar circumstance, in similar places, in similar positions. Much, much more enjoyable. And electric because that familiar buzz was there, multiplied because they were kissing.

Then she remembered her idea. Waited until the kiss had run its moment and they each took a second to breathe deeply and return to the world. And stared at him and said, "I have a suggestion and don't you dare refuse."

His eyes went wide. "Huh?" Because he'd been a thousand miles away. Or so close that she didn't want to think what that closeness meant.

She took a deep breath and touched his chin softly with her free hand the better to continue the buzz that came with touching him, the other hand being pinned beneath her, as she explained. "If you'll come to work for me, you can use the office in the kitchen to do your billing. There are pauses in the baking process and I promise to make sure you have plenty of them. You can simply duck into the office and do your medical billing. You'll be working two jobs at once and without the preparation of doing it at your place because you can leave your computer and whatever else you need here. In the kitchen. You'll earn double the pay for the time it takes to do one job." And she leaned on her arm and waited for him to react.

He did, after much thought and a couple frowns. "I do believe it can work."

"It can and it will."

A lazy grin spread across his face, she could see it in the dark in the shine of starlight on lips that had so recently belonged to her. "And we'll be working together. In the same kitchen. Day after day." His grin turned almost fatuous.

Her grin matched his. She didn't want to smile, she wanted to be serious and boss-like, but it didn't happen, she couldn't make it real, so she let her smile widen and found herself nodding infinitesimally. "Yep. Together. Hours at a time." She pulled back a bit. "Is that okay?" Knowing the answer but wanting to hear him say it.

"Better than okay." With a self-satisfied undertone, he leaned towards her once again and their lips tangled. For a moment. Until he pulled back reluctantly. "Of course, we'll have to set limits on the boss-employee relationship or nothing will get done. No muffins made to pay your bills, no medical billing done to pay my mine."

"Right." She nodded vigorously because, of course that's the way things would be. Should be. And the kisses of the last few minutes had been no more than an exploratory move between friends who happened to be bathed in starlight on a warm, summer night so they didn't mean anything. A rare occurrence that would never happen again because they were about to become boss and employee and everyone knew such romances don't work.

Though, to be honest, she'd enjoyed it a lot and if it should happen again – some day when things were slow and the sun was bright and they took a break in the tiny yard behind the commercial kitchen and they forgot that employer-employee relationship thing, well then, it would be okay with her. More than okay.

The next week, Abby and Bruce were invited to join other business owners at an impromptu picnic in the fairly new town park beside the river to celebrate a birthday. They never did find out exactly which business owner's birthday it was, but that didn't seem important.

Jerry's Pizza furnished pizzas and Abby and Bruce came up with a huge sheet cake that was laughable next to any professionally decorated cake but everyone devoured it greedily anyway, along with a ton of pop, fruit and many, many baskets of chips.

Abby and Bruce found themselves momentarily alone at one end of a table. "I feel terrible."

Bruce tipped his head. "Why? I'm enjoying myself."

"It's not that. We were invited because they all think we are regular business people. That we're going to be a permanent fixture in Johns Falls." She wiggled her shoulders and looked around quickly to make sure no one else was listening. "How will they react when they learn the muffin business is temporary?"

Bruce chewed his lower lip, then spoke in a kind of exploratory way. "I haven't noticed you filling out applications for jobs. Or asking anyone if they are looking for help. Or doing anything at all that people do who want a job." Narrowed his eyes and stared at her. Through her. "It looks to me like the muffin business is exactly what they believe it is. A permanent fixture in Johns Falls."

She hunched her shoulders. "But it isn't."

"Don't you like baking muffins?"

"I love it. I'd love to work in a bakery. But it'll never become a profitable year-around business. As soon as the summer people leave, as soon as winter comes, as soon as the snow starts to fly, I'll be broke."

Bruce, deep in thought, looked for a long time at the sky, the trees and a pair of eagles soaring above them. "I can't see the future so what you say may be true. But consider that Mickey's place is open year-around and so are the other restaurants that want what you make."

She said nothing but the idea of muffins being a year-around source of income was ridiculous. They were muffins, not gold.

But as time passed she accepted other social invitations from business owners because they were nice people and she liked their company. And Bruce was always there, watching her with raised eyebrows, his eyes questioning while he nibbled muffins and ate ice cream along with just about everyone else in Johns Falls.

She had a hard time keeping their relationship business-like and so did Bruce. Once when she was cleaning the kitchen as the sun dropped behind the trees because it was late, even considering the long summer evenings, he came up behind her and said, "Boo!"

She jumped. "You scared me."

He laughed and said, 'boo,' again, softly and somehow the word turned her insides to Jell-O. Or maybe it wasn't the word, maybe it was the gathering dark behind him, highlighted by the fire red sunset and the slight breeze that made his hair drift across his forehead and pressed his shirt against those considerable shoulders that were so capable in the kitchen.

And he leaned closer still and kissed her on the cheek. An experimental kiss that asked if another, deeper, more emotional kiss would be all right.

She didn't know how to respond. Her body wanted him, no doubt about that, but she was still his boss and, even though that would end as soon as she found a job, it hadn't happened yet. So she smiled and backed away imperceptibly and he knew what that movement meant and backed away too. And soon they were surrounded by other people because they were attending another celebration of something that was important to someone though she hadn't bothered to find out what because she was, after all, only a temporary member of the business community. And the moment passed.

But she remembered it for a long time and wondered what would have happened if she'd not backed away, if she'd let him know how she really felt. If they'd found a private place and let their feelings develop into whatever might come from a moment together.

And so the summer went. Days of work, nights of deep, exhausted sleep, and occasional fun times with other business owners. Bruce moved his computer into the office and Abby was amazed and impressed at how competent he was. He kept the door closed most of the time to keep flour and cocoa and other kitchen things from coating his computer so she didn't see him as much as she'd expected to – as much as she wanted to – but he seemed to know intuitively when his help was needed in the kitchen and he showed up. So things moved smoothly and everyone who ordered muffins or cupcakes or cookies got what they wanted when they wanted them.

Then autumn arrived and school started and summer vacationers thinned to those people without school-age children and, soon afterwards, to couples who came for the blazing colors of autumn, and then to just a few here and there for reasons no one knew other than that they seemed to prefer that time of year and the solitude it brought, and then the vacationers stopped coming altogether and the resorts closed and drained their water lines and everyone braced for the next season as a rising, cold wind blew the few remaining autumn leaves away and winter appeared overnight, like a ghost that was expected but came too early no matter the calendar date, and the snow that came so suddenly hadn't been forecast but came anyway, settling over everything and working its white ghost magic everywhere, whether the world was ready or not.

CHAPTER 14

Abby continued to be unaccountably, unexpectedly, busy. Business did slow down with the end of summer, but not enough to provide the idle, lazy days she'd expected, not enough to even close the business temporarily to go looking for a job. She was also busy enough that she didn't notice the change in the weather until waking one morning to white flakes falling straight down because in the forest there was no wind to blow them sidewise, though beyond the house, on the lake, she could see snow streaming horizontally across choppy waves that looked extremely cold.

She pulled the curtain fully aside to discover a white yard. White mounds capping evergreens, ready to slide down and pile on the ground around them. Here and there she saw small areas that were still autumn brown because they were sheltered from the white deluge. But they would soon be white also.

She took a deep breath and thought about the mile-long driveway and the thickly falling snow, wondering if her car would make it to the highway. It had to. She didn't have a choice, the kitchen in town awaited and so did customers who'd want baked goods whether it snowed or not.

So she showered in the shower she'd once thought she'd never use, dressed and grabbed a quick breakfast of cereal with milk and a glass of juice from the refrigerator she'd foolishly thought unnecessary. Then she took another glance outside. And gulped.

Those few autumn brown areas were gone. The world had turned completely white in the brief time it had taken her to get ready for work, and snow was piling higher and higher on the other side of the sliding glass doors on the deck overlooking the lake. It grew deeper as she watched. Not too much now, not yet, not too high as snow was measured and the driveway might still be manageable – she hoped it was -- but the white stuff kept falling, thick and full, obscuring distant objects, now hiding the lake that had been visible earlier.

She'd better get going if she wanted any chance at all of reaching town.

She unpacked the parka that was still in the box it had come in that spring and found a pair of sturdy, warm boots. Then she headed for the door and winter. And turned back before opening it in order to throw a couple outfits into an overnight bag just in case she ended up staying in town because the snow would be too deep to return home. Made sure London had enough food and water to last a long time and that his doggie door worked so he could come and go as necessary.

Then, taking a deep breath, she pulled the door open and stepped outside and stood stock still, frozen in place by the new world she now inhabited. The silence of winter enveloped her as surely as the snow was enveloping the entire world. She stood for a moment, listening, in thrall, enchanted, and knew that this was why she wanted this place so badly. For many reasons. The beauty of the day. The silence of the forest. And the childhood memories that came with all of those things. As she stood and let the snow coat her eyebrows and hair, memories of Christmases past danced in her head beside the new memories of quiet beauty she was making at the moment.

Until the silence was broken by the distant buzzing of a snowmobile somewhere that grew louder and still louder until Bruce appeared on a largish, rough-and-ready, very competent looking machine that he drove to the edge of the deck before cutting the engine to let the silence return.

He wore a helmet and carried a second one that he held out to her. "Here." He looked her up and down. "Nice parka. You look good in it. Got any Eskimo blood in you?" She smiled and shook her head as his inspection continued downwards. "Boots are excellent, you won't get cold in those but I hope you have some leggings because your jeans won't keep your legs warm during the trip to the highway where the truck is parked and when we reach town and a warm kitchen, the snow on them will melt and they'll become wet. Not fun." He tilted his head in a question. "So I repeat my question. Got leggings?"

"I didn't know I'd need any. I planned to drive to town."

He snorted his opinion of such an idea. "If you try to traverse that driveway and are lucky, you'll bog down in the yard before you even get started. The reason that'll be good is because you won't have far to walk back home." He shook his head at the very idea of trying to drive her small car through the rutted driveway in winter. "You won't make it to the highway, not in your car, probably not in my truck, not any way that I know of except by snowmobile." He patted the seat behind him. "So get something over those jeans, then hop on and we'll be off."

A few minutes later, ensconced in a pair of winter leggings that she'd found in the hallway beside the kitchen that had once belonged to someone, she had no idea who except that said person was much, much larger than she was, she found herself flying through the winter forest, behind Bruce with her arms around his middle and holding on for dear life. She'd have loved to admire the way the evergreens were now green and white instead of just green, how the forest floor was becoming a white carpet too thick to walk on but beautiful to behold but she didn't because it was all she could do to maintain her balance and not fall off as she held tighter and still tighter to the man in front of her and breathed a sigh of thankfulness for the warm electricity that his body sent backwards to her.

Until they reached the highway, where Bruce's truck was parked in a sheltered area. He whipped the snowmobile around a couple of times, almost unseating her, and then, evidently deciding it could simply replace the truck in its spot while they were gone, he came to a stop near a tall, solid tree that he soon chained the snowmobile to. In moments they were on their way, waiting for the cab of the truck to grow warm.

Then, as Bruce drove carefully along the highway

that hadn't yet been plowed and might as well have been a grassy field for all she could see the edges, she had time to finally admire the winter world. At least she watched it in wonder as soon as she decided that Bruce's driving on the highway was as careful as his mad dash through the forest on the snowmobile had been dangerous. Seemed dangerous but she didn't know that much about snowmobiles, perhaps his driving was sedate for such machines. She'd ask him, later that evening, when she was home and had survived this strange first day of real winter.

Later that day, when Bruce was finished with his medical billing and she'd reached a good stopping place with the muffin business, they broke for lunch at Jerry's Pizza. Half the town of Johns Falls was there, business owners, year-around residents, children too young for school and those who were homeschooled. Everyone, it seemed, had come to discuss the snow because it was important. Because the first snowfall was a major event that required serious consideration. And examination. And prognostication. The driveway to Abby and Bruce's places was one such topic.

"Old man designed the house well. None better. But that driveway." The speaker shook his head and most of the inhabitants of Jerry's did the same, making comments of their own about the sanity of building such a wonderful house in the woods and such a miserable driveway leading to it.

Bruce agreed. "So he made a mistake. No one's perfect."

Abby nibbled her pepperoni pizza and considered the remarks and could find nothing in them that wasn't accurate, though that wasn't how she remembered her grandfather, a man who rose from poverty to financial comfort by building homes that were solid, well designed, beautiful and practical. And they all had driveways, long and short, that got people to and from those houses without damage to vehicles.

So what was the story with the driveway to the house in the forest?

But, when she surfaced from her reverie, the conversation had moved on to how much snow was going to be on the ground when the current snowfall ended and whether the schools would close or not and how long it would be between this storm and the next and was this a predictor of the winter to come? Would there be snow higher than cars by the time spring arrived?

She said what she was thinking. "I love the snow. It's so pure, so white, so beautiful."

Most of the people at other tables nodded their heads, some saying something about it was lovely now but wait until March when they'd be sick of it. Sick of winter. Ready for spring green. A few just looked out the window at the white flakes still coming down, though slower now, and smiled.

"And I love Christmas in the forest. It's – special." She looked around to see how they felt and this time there wasn't a dissenting voice to be heard. Because Christmas in the north woods was special indeed.

One woman at a back table directed a question to Abby. "Will you be here for Christmas or will you head for your parents' place to be with family?"

She didn't know. Hadn't thought. Looked to Bruce to see what he'd be doing. Wondered if he'd be all alone in the forest and was that his usual Christmas? Or would he be with his parents, wherever they lived, in a forest somewhere, she assumed, because they'd left the modern world behind and the forest was a good place to do that.

His eyes were warm with Christmas thoughts but he said nothing, gave no indication of his plans as others in the pizza parlor said where they'd be and what they'd be doing and who they'd be with for the holiday and Abby's lack of an answer was forgotten in the general discussion of the holiday season that would be upon them shortly, or so it seemed now that winter had arrived. The atmosphere in the pizza parlor became almost festive as everyone pictured Christmas wreaths and other decorations draped around the walls.

On the way home that evening, in the truck, Bruce mentioned the lunch conversation. "Two flakes of snow fall from the sky and suddenly it's Christmas."

Abby considered the white world beyond the truck windows. "More than two flakes. A lot of flakes and they are still coming down. We'll hardly be able to navigate the yard, let alone the driveway and the highway, if more comes. We'll be snowed in and it's just the beginning of winter." She found that she was truly concerned.

Bruce just laughed. "Not with my trusty snowmobile. First day we can take time off from work, I'll take you for a ride through the forest that you won't forget. It's gorgeous."

She told him that she'd hold him to his promise because she'd love to see the woods in winter when the bears were hibernating, but only if he'd also promise to drive a bit slower than on their trip that morning and, surprised that she'd thought their ride had been anything other than sedate while wishing to accommodate her fear, he slowed down a bit.

CHAPTER 15

The ride never happened. Work and muffins got in the way. As they told each other, they had the whole winter to go for rides but customers wouldn't wait. So the days passed as did the first weeks of winter, with more snow and colder days and nights. The lakes froze over and ice crept closer and closer to the center of the river that snaked through town. Townspeople bet on when the river would be ice from shore to shore, but the swift-flowing current kept winning out against the cold and each morning water and choppy waves could still be seen, albeit less and less all the time.

And still they spoke of taking a ride through the wilderness. Until one morning bright and early as Abby waited as usual for Bruce to take them to the highway on his snowmobile and then on to town in his truck parked near the highway. It happened each and every weekday and she found herself humming softly as the familiar buzzing approached.

She waited as he came to a stop. Looked at him. Stared. Because something was different. Odd. Then he stopped the engine and, in the ensuing silence, she saw his expression and knew something was not only different, it was wrong. Very wrong.

"My mother broke her leg. Fell on the ice when one of the dogs went after a wolf that was getting too close to the house and she tried to stop the dog, fell on top of it, and then something went horribly wrong and she slipped as the dog dodged away from her and she ended up with a leg that's broken in at least three places. Maybe more."

"Oh no!"

"Don't know how bad it is because it just happened. She's in the hospital in Duluth being X-rayed as we speak." He licked his lips and held her gaze with those dark eyes, now worried sick. "I must go."

"Of course." The thought came crashing down that this meant he couldn't drive her to the highway. Couldn't drive her from the highway to town. Couldn't help at the kitchen. But he had to go to his mother.

What would she do? What *could* she do? Abby took a deep breath and silently swore that she would manage. Somehow. And that she'd do whatever she could to help Bruce and his parents get through this.

As it turned out, Bruce was way ahead of her and had thought things through, somehow, even as he'd prepared to go to his mother's side. "We'll take the snowmobile to the highway and the truck to town. A friend will lend me his car to go to the hospital. You use the truck and the snowmobile until I return."

It would work. "Call when you know how she is. Let me know. Please. Tell me your plans and what I can do to help."

His shoulders hunched. "The dogs –"

Of course. He had two huge dogs at his place that for a while would have no one to care for them. "I'll take care of them. I'll bring them here." His relief showed how concerned he'd been for his four-legged companions. "London is here already, two more dogs will just make things livelier."

He insisted that she drive the snowmobile to the highway and then the truck to town so she'd be experienced. Would know how to operate them both. "It's winter. There might be another snowstorm and the road might not be plowed. You should know the truck, the snowmobile, how to drive these particular vehicles on these specific roads in the winter."

She'd never thought of that. She'd driven many times in good weather but never in the dead of winter in bad weather and there was no guarantee of good weather in the near future. "I'll be fine. Slow and careful will get me there." But she held the steering wheel so hard that, when she tried to let up, her fingers refused to move.

The trip took twice as long as it should have because Abby was doing the driving, slow and careful as she'd said, but they reached town and the borrowed car in time for Bruce to head for Duluth and the hospital where his mother had been brought because the multiple breaks were bad and specialists must be involved.

Then Bruce took off and Abby spent the day alone, baking muffins and cupcakes and cookies and she managed because things had slowed down with the advent of winter. And because, soon after lunch,

Carolyn showed up, banging on the door of the commercial kitchen before opening it and walking in. "I hear you need help."

She went straight to the bulletin board where Abby pinned orders and inspected it without speaking. Then she nodded and headed for the huge cannisters of ingredients and, without a word, began making cookies. When she'd reached a stopping place, she turned to Abby. "Any help you need, just holler. The whole town will come running but I told them that the two of us – you and I – can probably manage just fine."

Abby almost cried. Had to shake tears away as she pulled hot muffins from the oven. "I think we can handle things, but I thank them anyway."

Carolyn gave a short, quick nod and continued, checking the recipes that were pinned beside the order sheets. "Looks like you have your ducks in a row. Good thing because you never know when something like this will jump out and bite you. Lesser businesses than yours have fallen apart because they weren't organized, but all I had to do was check out the bulletin board to know what needed to be done and how to do it."

By evening, they'd accomplished as much or more as she and Bruce normally did. Probably because they were working under pressure, wondering what was happening in Duluth, how long Bruce would be gone, how badly his mother's leg was broken, and what the future held for all of them.

Then, as Carolyn was slipping out of one of the huge aprons that kept their street clothes relatively clean while working, Abby's phone rang and it was Bruce. She held her breath, said a brief prayer, and answered.

"Mom's going to be okay." Thank God. "But it'll be a long, difficult recovery because of the multiple breaks. She'll be incapacitated for a long time, maybe several months. And she can't go home because the farmhouse is tiny and cluttered and all stairs." Abby took a deep breath thinking about the difficulties of someone with a badly broken leg living in a house with stairs. "So I'm bringing my parents home with me."

To another tiny, cluttered one-room house? Ridiculous! They'd bump into each other every time they turned around. And what about power? If Bruce only ran his generator a few hours a day because of concern that it couldn't take too many hours at a time, then what would his parents do? Use cold water? See by the light of candles? Wrap themselves in blankets all day long?

"Not your house." The words came unbidden and she heard Bruce suck in his breath as he prepared to say there was no other place and she spoke before he got a chance. "There is better place. My home. Bring your parents to my house. You know what it's like. They'll have all the comforts of a luxury motel and you know it and I won't let you refuse because your mother needs all the help she can get."

There was a long pause, then, in a cautious voice that showed Bruce was thinking things through. "They have two dogs and a cat. You already have three dogs at your place." Then, as he thought further. "But I can bring my three dogs home with me and then there will only be my parents' two dogs and a cat." Another pause. "Do you like cats?"

Abby burst out laughing. The question was so unexpected and so mundane considering the thrust of the conversation that it was exactly what was needed to break the stress that fairly hummed between them. "I love cats."

Then she, too, did some thinking. "You should move in with me too, until your mother is okay. To help with her. Carry stuff, maybe carry her. And like I believe I once said a while back when two more dogs moved in with me when you went to the hospital, bringing the total to three, the more the merrier and I mean it now when I say five dogs and a cat will be merrier still."

And they'd be temporary, though she didn't say so out loud because suddenly, unexpectedly, it was important that this happen. That Bruce and his parents come to live with her because the house in the forest was made for people. Lots of people. Tons of people. It could handle any crowd that came along, be it composed of humans or their four-footed friends.

But Bruce wasn't convinced it would work. "That's a lot of people and animals." She could hear the doubt creep into his voice. "It's a house, not a palace."

Abby chuckled. Laughed quietly. Then laughed out loud. "You haven't been upstairs or in the basement, have you?" A cautious 'no' was followed by silence as he waited for her to explain and she did. "Remember, there are four bedrooms upstairs, two on the main floor and three more in the basement, along with enough bathrooms for all those bedrooms to be full and no one to have to wait their turn for a shower. And, yes, there's enough hot water for everyone to take a shower at the same time."

There was an explosion of breath at the other end of the conversation, followed by a long pause during which she waited confidently because she knew what he'd say next. The only thing that made sense, given the fact that her grandfather had built the house to hold his entire large, extended family on special occasions. "Okay. We'll do it." Followed by, "But I owe you big time and don't you forget it."

She laughed again, a low, confident sound this time. "Don't worry, I can think of a thousand ways you can repay me and they all have something to do with muffins."

Bruce's mother spent two more days in the hospital, during which Bruce and his father gathered clothing and other personal items and two dogs every bit as huge as London, Paris, and Madrid, and a tiny, delicate, white cat, into his father's truck with his parents' snowmobiles in a trailer behind and then headed back to Duluth to pick her up and bring everyone and everything, including all four-legged family members, to Johns Falls, where Abby awaited with Bruce's truck.

Bruce's mother was a tall, slender, very tired woman with silver hair that fell below her waist that was tied back with a bright red bow that told the world that she was bent but not broken. She smiled wanly and turned out to be every bit as gracious as Abby's mother when the whole family was gathered because Grace Carr was the best hostess in the city.

Bruce's father was equally silver-haired and clean-shaven and looked every inch the college professor he once was and he took Abby aside and made sure they were welcome because he didn't truly believe it until she said so herself.

Then he peered at her – through her – and nodded

briefly and smiled widely in relief that things would work out and led the way to the beginning of the driveway where Bruce's snowmobile awaited with the sled that he had directed Abby to find behind his house that would transport all those belongings and his mother carefully, softly and safely to the house in the forest that her grandfather had built.

Even with three snowmobiles and a sled, it took a while to get everyone settled and then Bruce headed for his own place to pick up clothes and whatever else he needed for an extended stay. It was full dark by the time everyone gathered around the huge table except Bruce's mother who was enthroned on the soft couch as Abby dished up the crock pot meal that had been cooking all day because she'd had no idea when her company would arrive or how hungry they'd be.

Very hungry, as it turned out. Bruce's mother made a negative statement about hospital food and both Bruce and his dad said that Abby's cooking was excellent. Her comment that they were probably so hungry that they wouldn't notice flavor at all went unnoticed because they were too busy eating to hear what she said.

Then bedrooms were discussed, with the elder Merriweathers getting the second downstairs bedroom, of course, while Bruce and Abby took a tour of the upstairs and basement so he could decide which of the many remaining bedrooms he wished to inhabit, though he didn't care so long as the one he chose had a bed because that was all that was truly important, as he said through a yawn that emphasized the circles beneath his eyes. He suggested that the next day they declare a holiday from muffins in order to get everyone settled comfortably into their temporary quarters. Examining him covertly, Abby wholeheartedly agreed.

CHAPTER 16

The next morning didn't go as Abby expected. Instead of a leisurely breakfast followed by a general getting-to-know-one-another session, Bruce's father, Jake, whose name Abby hadn't known until yesterday, cleared his throat as she and Bruce were piling dishes in the awesome dishwasher that came with the house that she'd started using the day she discovered that it would be okay with her grandmother. His mother, Grace, watched, clearly wishing she could help because she was evidently the kind of woman who'd be horrified if anyone thought she was shirking her duty. Conflict clearly warred in her face as she tried to decide which was more important, helping to get the kitchen clean or staying off her leg.

When her husband cleared his throat, though, they all turned to hear what he had to say. And then wished they hadn't because everyone recognized his expression, the kind that all people wear when they are about to give out bad news. They all wished Jake Merriweather wouldn't speak, though, to be honest, they could also tell from his expression that what he was about to say was important. "You do know, Grace, that we'll be here for some time to come." He indicated her leg, huge in its cast and propped on a stool.

She considered it ruefully and nodded that she knew it was a major medical problem. Then, as she thought over his words, something changed. Her expression darkened, her eyes widened ever so slightly but enough that Abby noticed. And she held her breath for a few seconds before asking quietly – too quietly – "How long, exactly?"

Jake cleared his throat again, wishing not to say what he was about to say. "Till several weeks after Christmas."

His mouth was open to say more but the words were drowned out by Grace's mournful protest. "No! Not home for Christmas? That's not an option!"

His hands waved ineffectually in the air. "But dear –"

"I want to be home for Christmas. I *need* to be home for Christmas!"

"I know how you feel about home and Christmas, dear, but the doctors said – "

"Take me home, Jake! Take me home *now*!"

The room went still. Everyone, even the dogs, became statues witnessing the sheer misery of the woman with the huge cast. No one moved until Jake, clearing his throat for a third time, moved to his wife's side and enveloped her in his embrace. "I wish it was possible, dear, but healing takes precedent over home.

Just this one time, this one year. Just for this Christmas."

She leaned into his body and stayed there for what seemed a long time and was probably no more than a few seconds. Then she withdrew and straightened, composing herself as the others watched, plastering a smile on her face that fooled no one, and nodding shortly with lips pressed hard together. "I understand, Jake. I truly do and I am sorry for making a scene and I'm truly grateful to Abby for opening her lovely home for us so I can recuperate in comfort."

She shook her head and Abby thought a tear or two flew from her eyes and into the tense air as she tried to pretend she no longer cared about not being in her own home for Christmas. "I apologize for being a foolish old woman." She did her best to appear happy. "And I promise that I won't make any more fuss." She looked at Abby, smiling broadly with no happiness at all. "I thank you from the bottom of my heart for inviting us into your home." Then she added, "I just hope that my being here won't spoil your Christmas."

Abby rushed to assure her that she was more than welcome and that the more the merrier as far as Christmas in the forest house was concerned. Then, privately, she was glad she'd not yet made plans for Christmas because, what with the day-to-day operation of the muffin business, the holidays were the last thing on her mind. Now she knew that if she'd made plans, they'd have to be changed to accommodate Bruce's parents.

As she thought about the coming holiday, she glanced at a calendar and saw, with horror, that Christmas was coming faster than she'd thought possible. It was almost here. And what would she do for the holiday? And would it involve her parents? She always went home for Christmas? Could she leave the forest house to be with them without insulting the Merriweathers?

Robin Carr was a born hostess. Her parties were the envy of everyone in their circle and Christmas was her thing. Abby loved the Christmases her mother arranged. If Abby's mother was in the forest house, she'd manage a wonderful Christmas there, too, but Abby wasn't okay with asking because they already had plans.

She decided that her Christmas would happen in the forest house and if that made her parents unhappy, she expected that they'd at least understand. This year's holiday would consist of Abby, Bruce and his parents. She gulped, remembering the multitude of friends and family that was her usual Christmas and steeled herself for a quieter celebration because Grace Merriweather needed to be here and it would only be for one year. One Christmas.

Which could very well be her only Christmas in the forest, she knew that, because she was cavalierly ignoring the one cardinal, inviolate rule Grandma Maude had laid down for owning the place. She was no closer to self-sufficiency than when she moved in last spring. All she was doing was baking muffins.

She gave a mental gulp and decided that it didn't matter if, when the year was up, her grandmother decided she didn't deserve the house in the forest. Grace's healing was all that was truly important and everything else would happen as it was meant.

She looked around and realized that everyone else

was already starting to find things to do with themselves. Bruce followed his father into the elder Merriweather's bedroom to help him unpack, while Grace lay back against the couch cushions and closed her eyes in a pretend sleep. Abby decided the best thing she could do was disappear and give Bruce's mother time to compose herself after the shock of being told she wouldn't be home for Christmas.

She went into her bedroom and looked around for something to occupy her for a while but left the door open because she didn't think about closing it until she realized that Grace might want more privacy than an open door could provide, so she went back to close it. And that was how she saw what happened next.

Grace Merriweather was no longer reclining on the couch. Instead, she'd raised herself until she sat straight up. Stared at her leg, all wrapped in a cast, in clear anger, hatred, and frustration. Then she stared at her crutches. Then she leaned enough to grab both crutches in her hands and she threw them across the room as a low growl emanated from her mouth that told whomever might be listening that she hated them and all they represented. Totally. Completely.

The crutches hit the stone fireplace, bouncing off and flying to far, different parts of the room. No damage done but they were out of reach.

Grace Merriweather stared after them, her frustration gone with the impulsive gesture that now made her unable to go anywhere because she needed them to navigate. She stared after them. Closed her eyes in despair. Reached out for them, knowing as she did that she couldn't possibly reach them.

Glanced at the closed door to the bedroom where

her husband and son were putting things away. Wished she'd not thrown them because how'd she explain why she'd done such a thing? And started to scoot off the couch with the clear intention of retrieving them before anyone was the wiser.

Abby barreled out of her room and towards Grace. Pushed her back down on the couch. "Don't you move! Don't you dare move! You'll hurt yourself."

Grace Merriweather turned white as she realized that someone had seen her outburst. Then she sagged. "I know, but I can manage. You don't have to worry about me. I threw them and I'll get them myself. I've done harder things in my life than picking up a couple of expensive sticks. I can get them."

"How?" Abby put her hands on her hips and stared the older woman down while remaining so close that she couldn't move. "On your hands and knees, which is impossible with that cast? By hobbling and ruining all the hard work those wonderful doctors did?" She stuck her face into Grace's face and left no doubt that she meant what she said. "I will get your crutches if you will just sit back and do nothing. Nothing at all!" She backed slightly to see if Grace would stay where she was.

She stayed. She lay back, defeated, looking at the crutches and knowing she had no choice. But tears pooled that she angrily shook away. "I'm just a foolish old woman."

"You're not." Abby was horrified at Bruce's mother's thoughts and wished with all her heart that she had her own mother's ability to sooth things and people until everyone was happy. She knew that she didn't. But she thought back over a childhood of watching her mother and tried to think what her mother would do in such a situation. And she knew. "So now tell me what's really bothering you." Then, thinking she knew the answer. "Are you that homesick?"

It was the right question. As Abby quickly brought the offending crutches back to their previous place so no one would know anything had happened, Bruce's mother took a deep breath and Abby knew she was going to find out if she was right about why the older woman had thrown them across the room.

"I'm not exactly homesick." She looked around. "This is a beautiful house and it fits perfectly in its setting. It's a forest house and the fireplace is awesome and the lake beyond is a feast for my eyes." She took another breath. "It's not that I'm here, I rather enjoy sitting on this comfortable couch and doing nothing. But I don't want to be here for Christmas." She shrugged. "Christmas is the problem." Her eyes dropped so Abby couldn't see them anymore and read her thoughts. "I'm big on Christmas." Said as an apology.

"So?" Abby didn't understand. Lots of people were big on Christmas and didn't go around throwing crutches across rooms.

"I'm ready to enjoy my stay here while I heal. *Was* ready until I learned I'd miss Christmas." She shrugged her shoulders and knew what she'd said sounded wrong. "Christmas on the farm, that is. Christmas as I've come to know it since we moved there. Christmas with my special, Christmas things." Abby thought those shoulders were the most expressive she'd ever seen as the older woman raised her eyes again and let Abby see how important being in her own home at Christmas was to her. With her own Christmas things. "It's hard to accept even if it is only for one year."

Abby thought hard. What would her mother say now? How would she make the other woman feel better? Again, she drew on her childhood and asked, very carefully, "Exactly what about Christmas will you miss by being here instead of in your own home?"

Those thin, elegant, expressive shoulders hunched. "I won't have my beautiful, special Christmas things. I know it's foolish but I'm used to a tree cut from the forest, not from a lot in town. And the ornaments that we've collected – and some that we've made ourselves – over the years. And the decorations that we put up every year." She gave Abby a rueful but tiny smile. "You know. All the things that make Christmas special. Like everyone, I guess, because everyone has a version of Christmas that's right for them. My Christmas is right for me." She raised her arms in a gesture of frustration. "It's right because I love all my beautiful Christmas stuff." And she colored as if she knew how foolish she sounded.

Relief flowed through Abby and she vowed to thank her mother for the life lessons she'd got as a child that she'd not known she'd been learning. "I planned to cut a tree from the forest. It's what we always did when we had Christmas here. My grandmother wouldn't have it any other way. And as for Christmas stuff, what specifically will you miss?"

The smile grew somewhat. Not much but it was bigger than before. "There's a box." She shook her head. "No, there are three boxes to be exact. They are stored in the loft that Bruce slept in as a boy and they hold all my Christmas things." She bit her lip but it was to hide the smile that kept growing as she thought of the things that were dear to her. "I even labeled them. It says 'Christmas' all over them just because I felt like reminding myself how special they were when I packed them away."

Abby nodded, biting her own lip as she thought over what the other woman had said. She was about to say that maybe they could send someone back to the elder Merriweather's farm to retrieve those boxes when Bruce and his father came out of the bedroom with satisfied looks on their faces that said everything was where it belonged.

They looked from Grace to Abby and back, knowing something had happened while they worked but, as neither woman said anything, they let it go and suggested hot chocolate and a bird-watching party because a flock of small, yellow birds had circled the deck enough times to decide that it was where they wanted to be and were in the process of landing and everyone could watch the birds on the deck and the lake in the background at the same time, with the sun shining brightly as it raced across the brief slice of sky that marked a winter's day.

"Christmas is wonderful not only because it's Christmas but because it's when the days start getting longer," Bruce's father remarked to no one in particular as he helped his wife to a comfortable chair where she could watch the proceeding beyond the sliding glass doors. He caught Bruce's eye over her head as the two of them wondered what had happened that they would probably never be told.

Abby chose to keep them in the dark. For a while. But that evening, after Bruce's mother was in bed because she was healing, after all, and needed more sleep than most people, at least during this early stage of her recovery, she told them about the incident with the crutches and the conversation that had followed.

She dropped her hands between her knees and looked at them both. Stared hard. "How difficult would it be for one or both of you to return to the farm and get those boxes?"

Bruce and his father looked at each other. Smiled. And spoke simultaneously. "Not difficult at all." His father rose and started pacing excitedly, which told Abby that what was in those boxes was important to him, too, but he'd been way more concerned with his wife's recovery than the most wonderful Christmas things in the world. "I'll go tomorrow."

Bruce held up a hand. "No. Mom needs you here. But Abby and I head off to the kitchen in town every day. It's our job. It's Abby's business. If Abby can make muffins and cupcakes and cookies by herself tomorrow, then I can head to the farm and get those boxes." His grin spread across his face until Abby thought it might break in two. "And Mom will be happy."

Abby laughed. "I think that you and your dad will be happy too."

Bruce colored and muttered something about if mothers are happy, then everyone was happy. But Abby caught the glint in his eyes. The shine of past Christmases with cherished objects and the hope that this Christmas would have them once more couldn't be hidden no matter how he blustered.

She thought about that. Bruce was not only a man of action and a wonderful survivalist, he was a caring family member and that sensitivity sent something warm wending through Abby's whole self and she had to mentally shake herself to keep her attention on the people in the room with her.

As she did so, she wondered if this new, pleasing but odd sensation would change the tingling she still felt each time her body came in contact with Bruce's. And what it would feel like if it did.

CHAPTER 17

Two days later, Abby knew getting those Christmas boxes had been the right thing to do. The thing that, as much as or more than physical therapy, would bring Bruce's mother back to normal. To happiness. To Christmas joy.

Because, as soon as his mother spied the boxes on the table when she hobbled into the main room for breakfast, she gave a tiny, happy shriek and almost didn't eat in her eagerness to open the boxes and inspect each and every ornament and decoration before going on to the next one.

Jake Merriweather had to gently remove the boxes from her loving grasp and put them on the couch so everyone could have breakfast. Bruce and Abby, of course, had already grabbed quickly poached eggs while checking to see that they had everything necessary for the day's work in town. And dressing in the extra warm clothes that the trip along the driveway necessitated.

By now, Abby loved that trip. Bruce drove slower than during the first trip and Abby had grown accustomed to the feel of the wind their passage made and to the blur of trees whizzing by on either side and overhead as the snowmobile sped along the driveway. So she didn't mind the trip now, she loved it as she loved the green of evergreens, the only green in the north country once warm seasons ended. The pristine white everywhere. The shadows on that white that changed them and the entire winter landscape into something from a fairytale. But she was always first in the truck because it was warm and comfortable and she couldn't wait till it was on the highway and the heater kicked in.

That day at the kitchen, things went smoothly, as seemed to be the case during the winter. Abby was amazed that there were still orders even though tourists and summer people were gone. But the local population continued to eat out and they loved her muffins and other baked goods. And there were a few tourists at those resorts that were open all year who loved the fireplace at Mickey's Pub and the leisurely meals he served and the atmosphere he'd created of slow, relaxed decadence.

So they worked long and hard making muffins and other goods and found themselves making the return trip along that driveway in the dark. No stars or moon because the trees that met overhead blotted out the sky. No mysterious shadowed world on either side because the black was uniform. Only the lights on Bruce's snowmobile showed them the way. Without those lights, Abby realized, they'd not have been able to see their hands in front of their faces and would have quickly become lost. Then they made the last turn and the house in the forest appeared like magic and this time it was blazing with Christmas lights.

Looking at it, glad of the reprieve from the dark, Abby let out an involuntary cry. "It's beautiful. Your mother is an artist."

The house was no longer just another building in the forest. It was a Christmas house, complete with lights along the porch and two evergreens in the yard covered from top to bottom with colored lights. A manger scene nestled in the snow beneath one of the evergreens in a space that had been hollowed out of the mound of snow that had, until then, completely covered the bottom of the tree. And through the windows, more colored lights could be seen softly surrounding the huge stone fireplace, with candles on the mantel.

They put the snowmobile away in silence and entered the house in awe. Then Abby did the only thing that made sense at that moment. She went straight to Bruce's mother, hunched over her crutches and waiting to see how they'd react to the work that had been done in their absence. And hugged her as hard as she dared given that she didn't want to put the silver-haired woman back in the hospital with still more breaks.

"I hoped you'd like it," Grace Merriweather said in what was clearly relief. Had she actually thought someone would object to such wonderful decorations? "Jake helped." Nodding towards her husband who stood by the fireplace with his arms crossed. Waiting for their reaction. Smiling because that reaction had been what he'd hoped for, even as he harrummphed quietly because Abby suspected that he'd had a very busy, very physical day. Grace Merriweather couldn't do much, so he'd done a lot.

"I'm sure you're exhausted." Said mostly to Jake Merriweather but Abby managed to include Bruce's mother in the comment because the whole thing had been her idea, after all, and the crock pot meal that sent pangs of hunger through her stomach had probably been her doing, done while navigating a strange kitchen on crutches.

About the time that meal disappeared and peach cobbler was brought out for dessert because you can't have cupcakes all the time, Abby's phone rang. She frowned because she didn't get many calls in this northwoods place. Her friends were doing things without her as their lives slowly disengaged. So pretty much the only calls she received were orders for more muffins or recorded messages that her kitchen supplies were waiting to be picked up. But this phone number was wrong for any of those things.

"It's Grandma Maude." She could hardly get the words out and, seeing her anguished expression, talk around the table came to an abrupt halt. Jake and Grace Merriweather might not know the importance of Grandma Maude to Abby's life but Bruce did and all they had to do was notice his reaction to the news that Abby's grandmother had called for all talk to stop immediately.

They waited with bated breath as Abby spoke with her grandmother, not knowing why they were doing so but knowing – sensing – that this was of the utmost importance.

When Abby clicked the phone off and looked

around, they all leaned a bit closer to hear what she was about to say. Because she had news, that much was evident. "Grandma Maude is coming for Christmas."

Bruce's parents smiled because this sounded wonderful. Bruce gulped and, after a moment of getting used to the idea, asked cautiously, "And to check on how you're doing?"

Abby nodded, barely able to move her head. "She didn't say so but I think that's part of the plan." Her voice was scratchy and the elder Merriweathers looked to each other and then to their son for enlightenment and he told them about the terms by which Abby would – or would not – inherit the very house they'd spent the day decorating.

Grace Merriweather looked around at the lovely Christmas house she'd created and said, after thinking for a long time, "It doesn't look much like the kind of frontier home your grandmother was expecting, not after Jake and I spent a day putting up lights and decorations everywhere." She breathed deeply. "We can take everything down. We'll do it first thing in the morning."

The decorations were important to Bruce's mother. Very important. They could make or break the healing process. And that meant they had to stay.

So Abby shook her head so violently that the scrunchie that had held back her hair at the kitchen flew halfway across the room. After retrieving it and pulling her hair once again through the loop, she bit her lip, looked around, stood a bit taller than she'd thought possible for a five-foot-two woman to stand, and said clearly and with no possibility of being mistaken, "The decorations stay. Every single one. Because they are beautiful and this is the way this house should look for Christmas and as long as it's my call – and until I'm told otherwise, it *is* my call – I want this place to remain the most beautiful Christmas house in the world."

"But the terms – " Grace Merriweather waved at the brightly lit room and the trees beyond the window. "So much electricity – "

"Everything will stay," Abby said firmly, knowing as she said the words that they were right. If her grandmother decided she wasn't living up the terms of the agreement, so be it. Until then, though, they'd have the most beautiful Christmas possible. And afterwards? She'd deal with moving back to the city and giving up her dream of owning the forest house when – and if – it happened.

Grandma Maude didn't come immediately because the Caribbean was warm and comfortable and she'd made a new life with her old friends and was reluctant to return to cold weather and snow and ice any sooner than necessary. But she was determined to spend Christmas with her granddaughter in the place where she'd grown up and so one day she got on a plane and flew to the Twin Cities, where she got on another, smaller plane that took her to Bemidji, where she got a bus that took her to Johns Falls where Abby and Bruce met her with his truck because it and his father's truck were the only vehicles available to bring her to the start of the driveway, where he had a sled filled with warm blankets for her to ride in along the driveway that her husband had, for some reason, not had made well enough to plow during the winter.

When they arrived at the house in the forest,

Grandma Maude didn't go inside immediately. Instead, she walked back through the snow to get a better view of the panorama spread before her. The evergreens covered with lights, the manger scene, the blazing colors seen through the windows.

She tilted her head to one side and then the other the better to grasp what had been done. And she smiled. Nodded to herself. And told Abby and Bruce that this was exactly, precisely, the way the house was meant to be during the Christmas holidays. With which she climbed the stairs, crossed the porch, went inside, introduced herself to the elder Merriweathers and congratulated them on doing such a wonderful job of decorating. Then she found a comfortable chair and dropped into it, leaned back against the soft cushions and said to no one in particular that it was nice to rest after her long trip.

That night, Abby was too keyed up to sleep. In her pajamas, she padded to the window and sat on the broad sill, looking out over the lake in the moonlight. The house was dark, the Christmas lights having been extinguished for the night. As she considered the moonlight on the frozen lake that now resembled a broad field that awaited ice fishing shacks and cross-country ski tracks, both things she'd not yet had time to enjoy, she wondered how much longer she'd be able to stand there and look over the lake. If she'd be there next winter.

Because, though Maude Carr approved of the Christmas decorations, she'd said nothing of Abby herself. Whether she approved of the life her granddaughter was carving out in the wilderness. Or not.

If she would give her granddaughter more time to find a job because so far she'd been too busy baking muffins to find the job that would enable her to meet the terms of the agreement. Or not.

If she'd ever own the house in the forest that she'd come to love during this eventful year even more than she had loved it as a child. Or not.

It was long after midnight when she finally returned to bed and managed a short spell of fitful sleep. The next day, at the kitchen in Johns Falls, Bruce noticed the circles under her eyes and that she moved slower than usual, but he said nothing, stepping in to grab the muffins from the oven because she yawned when the timer went off, pulling more strawberries from the freezer himself though she normally did so and all without comment, setting them aside to thaw because she'd forgotten them. Pulling her against his chest halfway through the afternoon and telling her that everything would work out for the best. Not saying that she'd get what she wanted – the house in the forest – because he couldn't know that she would. They both knew she might not.

And, even as tired as she was, that tingling that she felt whenever they touched, made her feel better. Warmer. Nicer. As if, even if she didn't get the title to the house in the forest, life would still be okay.

She dropped her head to his chest and simply breathed in the essence that was Bruce and was thankful that he was there. That he was in her life. That he understood.

That evening, she decided it was a good thing she'd had that brief moment of encouragement. She needed it. Because once again, at the exact moment dinner ended, her cell rang. She glanced at the number. It was her mother.

"Hi, dear." Her mother's cheery voice came to her. Not that her mother was ever other than cheery, it was her nature, if her mother frowned, things were very bad, so the tone of voice told her nothing. "How are you doing, dear?"

Abby answered cautiously, knowing it would take her socially adept mother a while to get around to the reason for the call. But, after checking on Abby's health, friends old and new, and what was happening in Johns Falls, she said innocently enough, "I hear your grandmother Maude is there."

Grandma Maude was the reason for the call? But why were Grandma Maude's whereabouts important? Abby's mother continued. "And I hear she's going to be there through Christmas." A pause, then, "And that you have some other company also."

"Yesssss…...." Abby still didn't know where this call was headed.

"And there are still empty bedrooms?"

"Yesssss……" More information but still no decisive reason for the call.

Her mother laughed, the silvery sound Abby remembered from childhood. "That's good because your dad and I are hoping we can use one of those bedrooms and come for a visit." A pause for Abby to take in what her mother had said, then, "And stay through Christmas." Another pause before she continued. "Like old times."

Abby's phone was quiet, the others around the table couldn't hear both sides of the conversation but they knew from her expression that something major was happening. Again.

Abby finished the talk with her mother and as softly as possible clicked the phone off. Took a deep breath. And said, "Mom and Dad are coming. Next week. And they'll stay through Christmas."

Bedlam broke out. Questions were asked but not answered. Bedrooms were considered and it was made very clear that the elder Merriweathers were not going to move upstairs no matter how they insisted so Abby's parents could have the bedroom next to their daughter because a broken leg trumped any parent-child relationship.

As for Grandma Maude, she started smiling and kept it up until her face almost split. "Just like old times. The whole family in the house where I grew up. In the forest. An old-fashioned Christmas and, since we loved company and had a lot of it, having the Merriweathers here makes it that much better." She took a deep breath, closed her eyes in ecstasy, and leaned even farther back in her cushy chair. "I love Christmas here in the forest."

Only Abby was quiet, wondering how hard it would be to keep a happy face in front of all these people she loved and those she was learning to love if – or maybe it was more realistic to think *when* – her grandmother informed her that, sadly, she wasn't living up to the terms of their agreement and so, as soon as Christmas was over, she should pack her bags and return to the city where she belonged.

On the other hand, her grandmother loved her. She might give her the house anyway. Or at least she might let her stay until spring. Abby hoped so as she pasted on a huge smile and went to prepare still another bedroom for occupancy.

CHAPTER 18

Abby's parents had been to the house in the forest many times and for many Christmases. After all, it was where Abby's dad had spent much of his childhood and the memories were thick and full and they knew everything about the house, the land, and the driveway. Most of all, they knew the driveway.

So they came in their huge SUV that could easily hold nine people and that might possibly make it through the snow-packed driveway to the house itself. But, being sensible people, they left it beside the trucks already parked in the small area beside the highway and rode the rest of the way on snowmobiles driven by Bruce and his father, with luggage and the elderly family dog on a sled behind Bruce. Abby's mother loved dressing well, even in the wilderness, so there were a number of suitcases and there was no thought of leaving their dog behind. He was, after all, part of the family and knew the forest house well and would most likely love meeting all the other animals that were already there.

It was still light out when they entered the house. Abby's mother stepped through the door, then stopped and simply stared at the transformation that Bruce's parents had wrought. The ornaments. The decorations. It was a total Christmas package. "It's lovely," was all she said but her voice told everyone how beautiful she considered everything to be.

Being the gracious person that she was, she went straight to Bruce's mother and hugged her lightly. "I believe we owe all this beauty to you." She turned and nodded to Bruce's father to include him because, after all, he'd obviously done all the heavy lifting.

There was a leisurely dinner followed by talk late into the night, with Grandma Maude retiring in the middle because, as she said, she was old enough to decide for herself when it was her bedtime. Then, one by one, the others retired until only Abby and Bruce were left in the huge living room, along with an assortment of dogs and one cat looking over a lake that was dark because there was no moon and the stars alone didn't light the world enough to turn the snow-covered lake into the bright opening in the forest that it often was.

They didn't pretend not to be thinking about Grandma Maude and the forest house that she might – or might not – give to Abby. "She didn't mention the agreement?" Bruce asked cautiously.

"Not yet." Abby let her concern show because Bruce knew everything about the agreement. There was no reason to hide her fear from him. "Do you think that's a good sign or bad?"

He shrugged because he knew no more than she

did. But he moved to her, gathering her into his arms, pulling her against him as they both turned to watch the world beyond the sliding glass doors. The pack of dogs and one small, white cat gathered around them as if knowing how Abby felt and wanting to ease her pain.

And that pain actually was eased by both the animals that surrounded them and the familiar fizz that touching Bruce always brought, along with the something else that had been added lately that she couldn't define because she didn't know what it was or where it came from or why she felt it. But she did, and it grew with each touch and the warmth of his body, the pulse of his heart that she could both hear and feel as her head lay on his chest. The reassurance that his presence provided.

At last she spoke, trying to sound brave but not sure she was managing. "It'll be alright either way. No matter what she decides." Because at that moment, touching him, feeling his strength, she believed it. And she could be alright if she had to return to the city. Might be aright if she worked on it.

"Are you sure?"

She thought about it, about how she'd actually feel if her grandmother took the forest house away because she'd not lived up the agreement and she no longer had Bruce's solid presence to protect her from disappointment. As she listened to his heartbeat, her determination not to wilt no matter what the future held grew until she felt the truth of her next words. "Yes, I'm sure. It'll be hard, but I'll be okay."

"Good girl." He squeezed gently and then let her go, moving silently to the stairs and his own room as she remained behind with the dogs and cat for what could be one of the last nights she'd gaze on the scene that had been with her since childhood. Because she had no clue what Grandma Maude would decide. Or when she would make her decision. She'd said one year but why had she come now if not to see how things were going and, as long as she was here, why not either give Abby the house or not?

The next morning, everyone slept in after their late night until they all straggled out and sat around and nibbled rolls for breakfast because no one felt like cooking. Midway through, Grandma Maude informed them that she'd decided to treat them all to dinner at Mickey's Pub and Eatery so they'd best not have a huge lunch.

It would be a late afternoon meal instead of dinner at the usual time because dark came early in the north country in early winter and, even eating in town in the afternoon instead of waiting for a more normal dinnertime, they'd return along the driveway in the dark.

Grandma Maude had lived in the north country long enough to know that traversing that driveway through the wilderness in the dark was more than interesting. But she wanted to go to town during her stay and today was as good a day as any. More than that, she wanted to do something for everyone and a meal out would work. And she wanted to see Johns Falls and find out how her childhood home was faring.

So they fed the dogs and the cat, made sure there was water for all, and set off for town, bundled beyond recognition for the snowmobile portion of the trip with nice clothes beneath their winter outerwear that would be uncovered when they were in the Carr's toasty warm

SUV that held so many people.

Mickey's Pub wasn't busy at that time of the afternoon. Less than a dozen tables were full, mostly of families with small children who shouldn't stay up too late so had come for an early dinner as had Abby's group, but there were also two local retired couples and a few more that Abby didn't recognize and thought might be stray tourists who'd come for a winter visit.

Mickey was talkative, especially when he realized that his newest group included Maude Carr. "We go way back," he said to the family as he led them to a large table that had been formed by pushing two smaller ones together and was right in front of the fireplace "My parents went to school with Grandma Maude and I spent a lot of time at the forest house growing up." He hugged the elderly woman. "I'm so glad to see you again."

As dinner progressed, Mickey returned several times and each time he joined the group for as many minutes as he could spare from the kitchen. And he made sure Maude Carr knew that his featured desserts were provided by her granddaughter.

Grandma Maude asked to see the dessert cart. When it arrived, she looked it over and nodded approval of the cupcakes and cookies on display, ignoring the few other desserts that shared space with Abby's creations.

As she examined everything, a gleam came into her eyes and, before anyone knew what was happening, she rose and took Mickey aside. They spoke for a moment, with Maude asking a question none could hear. Mickey listened, nodded and made a beeline for the kitchen.

Soon he reappeared with what Abby knew was the

largest dessert cart in the place, the one that was normally brought out only for meetings and other large gatherings. It was filled to overflowing with Abby's cupcakes, cookies and muffins. And nothing else.

Mickey expertly maneuvered the huge thing to their table and presented it to Grandma Maude with a flourish. "Is it to your liking?"

Grandma Maude looked it over and nodded. Then she rose and took the cart, saying, "I'll be back in a bit. There's something I wish to do." And, pushing the cart before her, she headed for the nearest occupied table.

A family with two small children watched her approach in surprise and puzzlement as Abby wished she could sink through the floor. Instead, she listened carefully as her grandmother explained to the family that she wished to treat them – and all the other diners in the Pub – to the treats that her granddaughter had made. And she wanted their honest reactions when they'd sampled everything that appealed to them. Then Grandma Maude stood back and waited.

The parents hesitated at this strange request but the kids weren't a bit shy. They dove in and soon had sampled every kind of cookie and two cupcakes each and were heading for the muffins when their parents said they'd had enough because they'd be up all night with upset stomachs if they kept going. Then the parents, hesitant at first, but with more and more enthusiasm as they continued, sampled the contents of the dessert cart for themselves.

Grandma Maude asked for their opinions and the family didn't hesitate to say they were among the best desserts they'd ever had and to ask how to get more later because, though they surely would ask for more the next time they dined at Mickey's, they'd also like to buy some from the store where they were for sale when they were next in town.

In triumph, Grandma Maude said that they could find some of her granddaughter's creations at the candy store and possibly would find all of them there in the coming summer.

With a smile and a nod, she moved to the next group of diners, who'd been watching and were already looking forward to something special and waiting for the dessert cart to come their way.

Eventually every diner in Mickey's Pub had been treated to desserts made by Abby and Bruce and when Grandma Maude returned to their table, she resembled a conquering heroine, pushing the almost empty cart before her, in spite of the fact that it had been refilled three times during her trip around the Pub.

"They liked everything." She sighed happily, her smile broad and satisfied. "In fact, they loved every single item on the cart." She looked at Abby. "They loved your creations, dear granddaughter."

Abby gulped, feeling the weight of the combined stares of every single customer in the restaurant. "They are your recipes, Grandma."

One of the nearest diners, the father of the kids, overheard and called out. "Really? Old recipes and a great baker. What do you call your business, anyway? We want to know so we can spread the word."

Abby turned to stone. "I don't have a name for it." She tried to explain, stumbling over her words. "I never got around to choosing one." Because the muffins weren't a business, they were merely an interim income producer until she found a real job. But she couldn't say that, not here, not now.

Another diner, a retired woman two tables away, joined in. "Did I hear you say they are your grandmother's recipes?" Abby nodded as everyone's attention moved to her grandmother. "Well, I must say that they are wonderful." She checked out Grandma Maude from head to toe. "You've been around for a few years, I'd guess, and so have the recipes." When Grandma Maude nodded, she continued, "Old recipes are the best. Everyone knows that any grandma's recipes are preferred over all others."

The first man, the father of the kids who might have tummy aches later that night, looked straight at Grandma Maude. "So what's your name, if you don't mind? I'd like to personally thank the woman whose recipes are about to become a part of our lives."

Surprise showed in Grandma Maude's face. This was something she'd not expected when she asked Mickey for the dessert cart. But she rose to the occasion and told them that her name was Maude and that she was Abby's grandmother.

"Grandma Maude." The father rolled the name around his mouth a few times. "It has a ring to it."

A third diner, three tables away, jumped in with, "And she makes muffins, too. There were some on the cart but I've had them before if I remember correctly. I bought some at the Farmer's Market and they were amazing. I came back for refills several times." He thought a moment, then sighed wistfully and said, "I loved Grandma Maude's muffins."

The father of the two children snapped his fingers. "That's it. Grandma Maude's Muffins. A name with a ring to it."

The third speaker chimed in again, waving the remains of a cookie in the air. "And more because she makes more than just muffins."

The original man said, "Grandma Maude's Muffins and More." He gestured for the remaining diners to join in the conversation. "What do you think? Have we named this young woman's business? Grandma Maude's Muffins and More?"

There were a few cheers and, without knowing quite how it happened, Abby was informed that she was now the proud owner of a business named Grandma Maude's Muffins and More. As she shrank into herself, wondering how this had happened while knowing exactly how – her grandmother acting like a grandmother who was proud of her granddaughter's accomplishments and went out of her way to show it – she managed a wan smile and thanked the whole of Mickey's Pub, which by then included the kitchen staff who were watching with interest from the open door to the kitchen and trying hard not to laugh.

When things had settled somewhat, which was when the kitchen staff had returned to work and the other diners to their own concerns, Grandma Maude dropped once more into her seat and looked around. "That was interesting. And informative. And fun."

She turned to Abby, who by then was a wilted mess who wanted nothing more than to disappear completely and never be heard from again. "And it's time I said what I came all the way from the warm Caribbean to say. That I'm proud of you. Of the way you stepped up and did what I asked. Kept as true to the pioneer way of life as is possible in today's world and, along the way, figured out a way to make a living –

more than a living, a business -- so you can remain in Johns Falls permanently."

She cocked her head and her eyebrows rose in rueful acknowledgement of the truth of her next words. "To be honest, I never expected that your way of making a living would involve a business using the old recipes from when I was a child." Then her face returned to normal. "But I'm so glad it turned out this way because owning your own business is special and a part of me is in that business."

Her eyes misted. "Your grandfather believed passionately in his business. Couldn't have stood working for anyone else. And look how successful he was." They all knew where the money to refurbish the house in the forest had come from.

Then she added, as if it was almost an afterthought. "By the way, the house in the forest is yours as soon as I can get the paperwork drawn up. Forget the one-year stipulation, you've shown that you not only want to live here, but that you can do so quite well."

Abby was so stunned that she couldn't speak and everything she might have said was crowded out by the thought that somehow, amazingly, against all odds, even against her own plans, she'd become a business woman who was about to have her most fervent wish come true. To own the house in the forest.

No longer was she waiting for a job to open up, she was on her way to making Grandma Maude's Muffins and More into the best business possible. And all because Bruce suggested she make a few dollars selling muffins at the Farmers' Market.

She caught his eye and the tiny smile that he couldn't quite hide said he knew exactly what she was thinking. But then, he usually knew what she was thinking.

The group knew Abby needed time to think, so they left her alone during the ride in the Carr's SUV back to the snowmobiles and the subsequent trek through the pitch-black wilderness to the forest house that, when they finally reached it, glowed with the Christmas lights and the moonlight because the moon had finally come out in full glory and gilded everything with its silver shine.

CHAPTER 19

Bruce's parents went straight to bed. So did Abby, who wouldn't admit she was exhausted by the day's events and the thoughts that swirled through her mind until she found herself putting her mittens in the refrigerator and decided the wisest course of action was to just give up, give her grandmother an extra hard hug and disappear into her bedroom. She was asleep less than a minute after her head hit the pillow.

In the morning, she learned her parents and grandmother had stayed up far into the night, talking. About her. Asked Bruce all sorts of questions about the business because he was involved and could answer them almost as well as Abby herself. And had come to a decision.

"We are going to buy the commercial kitchen in town that you use." They didn't wait for her reaction before continuing. "So Grandma Maude's Muffins and More can get off to a good start. So you won't have to worry about the kitchen you use being sold out from under you."

Abby's first thought was that their offer was wonderful. Her second was that they didn't have to do anything because getting the house in the forest was more than most people ever got. Her third was that accepting the kitchen in addition to the house would be wrong, totally wrong, because she needed to stand on her own two feet and discover what she was made of. So she took a deep breath, said goodbye to an easy entry into the world of business ownership, and said, "Thanks, but no thanks."

Three mouths dropped a mile as they asked why not, but they accepted her explanation that she wanted to do as much as possible on her own and didn't want – or need – to be propped up by family, no matter how loving or well-intentioned their offer. But they were concerned and made sure she understood that if at any time she needed anything, all she had to do was ask.

After all, she was the only child of a successful lawyer and the granddaughter of an equally successful contractor and that meant they could make life easy for her. She smiled and said she'd figure things out on her own.

They all gulped and later, in private, told each other how proud of her they were and how they hoped she knew what she was saying because it was sinfully easy to fail in business. Any business. And they had a long, detailed conversation about how to monitor her progress so they could step in if one of the many pitfalls to success tripped her up.

None of them wanted that to happen because there were few means of making a living in a small town in northern Minnesota so if Grandma Maude's Muffins and More failed, she'd have a hard time finding another source of income and that would never do, not for a relative of theirs, and it wouldn't happen if they knew what was going on in time to step in and help out. So they cornered Bruce and made him promise to spy on Abby just enough to let them know if problems surfaced. Bruce gulped but, surrounded by three determined people who wouldn't take 'no' for an answer, agreed.

They didn't believe him, he was clearly lying, he'd never tattle on Abby behind her back, but it was the best they could do so they accepted his promise and hoped it would be enough to goad him into action if something went wrong.

Then, comfortable with their world and their plan, they went outside to admire the falling snow that was piling softly on top of the old snow with no wind to push it sideways, giving the house and the whole area an even deeper covering of white on white than before. There was no way the Carr's SUV could make it along the driveway now.

The few days left before Christmas passed quietly enough and they all piled once more on the snowmobiles and sleds to head for the Christmas Eve service at the church in town. The sky was cloudy enough to hold even the faint starlight at bay so they'd return in full dark, the kind that made it impossible to see a hand in front of a face. It would be a slow trek back to the house in the forest.

The ceremony was everything they could have wanted and more and there'd be treats and hot apple cider when they got home, thanks to Abby and Bruce bringing cookies and cupcakes from the kitchen in town after their last day of work before taking a Christmas break.

Changing from the SUV to the snowmobiles was slow work, involving pulling on warm outerwear in the full dark of night but, once everyone was warm beyond any possibility of a chill during the ride to the house, they piled onto the snowmobiles and began the trek through the forest that was dark and mysterious at that time of night.

Midnight came while they were still moving single file along the driveway that was now no more than a single snowmobile track in the snow. Abby, behind Bruce, tapped him on the shoulder and leaned close as he half turned to hear what she said. "Merry Christmas, Bruce."

She felt rather than saw his smile as he mouthed, "You too," before he turned back because it was dark, after all, and careful driving was essential. But she thought she felt his smile for the remainder of the trip.

How that could be she didn't know. Didn't wonder about it. Just accepted it, like she'd come to accept the faint but very real frizzle of electricity that went through her every time they touched. There was no explanation for that, either, but the sensation was as real as the surrounding forest.

Or was there an explanation? A reason as old as time? As she leaned into his broad back and greedily took more of the familiar sensation into her body, she suddenly realized that she knew what caused it. Why it happened. How it had come to be.

She was in love with Bruce and she couldn't imagine why she'd not figured that simple fact out earlier.

Love!

But, darn it anyway, Bruce didn't love her back. If he did, she'd know it. Wouldn't she?

She considered the question as they passed unseen evergreens on either side with quick glimpses of more ahead in the winking light from the snowmobile's headlights. Of course she would. She'd know.

Or perhaps not because Bruce was sometimes difficult to read so she couldn't be sure how he felt about anything beyond his love of the north woods, his parents, and three very large dogs. His background was so totally unlike hers that there was no commonality there. And his experiences in life were also different. So there were things about him that she was sure she didn't see in their daily life together even though they spent many hours in each other's company.

So he could be in love with her and she'd simply missed it because it showed in some way she didn't know.

Nope, she decided after thinking on it for a bit, she'd know if he was in love with her – she'd sense it -- and he wasn't.

So she'd better figure out how to live out her life as his next door neighbor and coworker and be happy with what she'd have of him. Which, as she thought about it, was a lot, just not as much as she'd wish with someone she loved.

So she simply leaned closer into his back as they continued their slow trip through the forest and wished it would last forever as she absorbed the essence that was Bruce and took it into herself to remember later, when their bodies would no longer touch.

Then the trio of snowmobiles reached the clearing

that held the house in the forest and Abby's breath left her at the true awesomeness of the picture it made. The house itself against the white snow that somehow was white even without the stars or moon. The Christmas lights strung everywhere, inviting them in. The lake beyond, a space that was felt more than seen, a lighter shade of black in the black night. The snow piled everywhere, white and pristine and clean and so beautiful the sight made her blink tears away.

The house was everything she'd ever wanted and more. And, as she let her gaze wander everywhere, she noticed the three-car attached garage that was empty because the vehicles were parked at the highway. Even the snowmobiles weren't parked in the garage, Bruce having chosen to leave them, instead, beneath the sturdy awning her grandfather had built for just such occasions, protecting them from snowstorms even as it protected people.

The garage was not needed. In fact, it was almost laughable how seldom it had been used in all the years she'd come to the house in the forest. No reason to put cars in it in the summer and no cars to put in it in the winter.

But it would make a great commercial kitchen. Heated – of course, her grandfather wouldn't have considered not heating any part of the building – and clean as a whistle because it was almost unused. She wondered how difficult – and how expensive – turning the garage into a commercial kitchen would be.

She could purchase the equipment from the kitchen in John's Falls if Carolyn would sell it. She'd ask Carolyn what was involved in building a commercial kitchen. Carolyn would know because she knew everything.

Having so decided, Abby came back to the real world of snow and Christmas lights and a family that had already dismounted from their snowmobiles and was staring at her as she sat all alone on the seat of hers since Bruce had long since joined everyone else in heading for the house. And smiled.

"I think I'll see about turning the garage into a commercial kitchen so I can work right here in the forest."

Everyone's eyes went large. Then they looked at each other. Then they, too, smiled and nodded and soon were discussing the various possibilities and trooping into the empty garage to see what could be done, though not one of them knew what was required. But they did know what the kitchen in town was like and they spent a good hour mentally transferring everything that was in it to the garage.

Yes, they all decided, it could work and both Abby's parents and her grandmother volunteered to co-sign if the bank wouldn't give her a loan on her own credit because she was, after all, a newcomer to town and new to the world of business. Abby vowed to talk to the bank without letting them know because, if they knew when she applied for a loan, they'd all be there beside her and would stare at the banker with daggers until he gave her money.

Family was nice. Family was wonderful. And sometimes family was a bit too much. For some reason she couldn't fathom but knew was important to her sense of self-worth, she wanted to do this without help so she told everyone that there was an entire winter to think things through and deal with loans and such, while privately deciding that the first week in the new year would be a good time to visit the bank.

The family went to bed and so did Abby but she couldn't sleep. Too much went through her mind. Bruce, mostly, but also the concept of a work space right in the house in the forest that she loved so much that was actually going to belong to her. She felt everything in waves going through her body and finally gave up any pretense of sleep and returned to the main room and a half dozen dogs sleeping in various places and one small, white cat curled up on the mantle in the center of an arrangement of greenery and pine cones.

The weather had changed while she'd been in her room. The clouds had dissipated. The moon and stars were out and the sky glowed with their brilliance and the northern lights blazed. She padded to the sliding glass doors and gazed over the property that would soon belong to her and was moved almost to tears. Surely the first Christmas had been on a night like this. She lifted her eyes to the sky and gave it a careful perusal just in case there was an unusually brilliant star up there somewhere shining down on a manger. But the sky was a uniform blanket of twinkling stars.

"Hi." She jumped. "Just me. Bruce. I heard something. Thought it was the dogs and decided to check."

"Just me." She measured the distance between them and wished it was less because she wanted that electricity that came with touching him and knew it wouldn't happen. Not now. Not tonight. "You can go back to sleep."

He smiled. She felt the smile as she'd felt it on the snowmobile, rather than seeing it in the dark because his large, competent form was indistinct and neither of them made a move to turn on a light. Enough came from the sky outside, there was no need for more.

They moved to those doors and stood for the better part of an hour looking out on the winter world, not speaking, not touching. Until Bruce moved. Reached for her. Pulled her to him and she went willingly, gladly, greedily, and they stayed that way, with her using his body's heat to cocoon her from the coolness of the room, of the night beyond.

And then, in silent agreement, they returned to their own rooms and this time Abby wisely carried the white cat to her bed and curled around it's purring, compliant form and slept.

CHAPTER 20

Christmas day was warm and friendly and wonderful, with a meal both prepared and shared by everyone and gifts that had somehow materialized in spite of the fact that shopping trips to town were so difficult that no one had suggested any.

Bruce had used his artistic talents to provide everyone with pictures on birchbark. Abby almost cried when she saw hers, a picture of herself on the deck in the summer sun. But she'd done her bit as well, baking treats for everyone that were presented in baskets she'd purchased just for the occasion that Grandma Maude, when she opened hers, suggested would make wonderful gift baskets to sell in the candy store in town.

Everyone laughed because it was becoming clear that the construction business Grandma Maude's husband had started that had been so successful had been a two-person operation and the second person had been Grandma Maude herself. The woman was a born entrepreneur.

And so it went, with gifts for all and a comfortable, roaring fire reminding everyone that, though it was cold outside, it was warm and friendly inside. It was a lazy day that Grace Merriweather said was all she'd hoped for and had been afraid she'd miss when she broke her leg, and that Grandma Maude said reminded her of the years during which her entire, extended family had gathered for Christmas at that very house in the forest and had a blast.

As the day wore on, talk changed from Christmas to the venture Abby was about to undertake. Turning the garage into a work space. Bruce had one caveat. "The driveway. It's awful and everyone will have to travel it to get to the workspace."

Abby nodded thoughtfully. "Delivery people will hate it."

"Unless we pick up supplies in town when we're bringing orders to customers. That could work."

Abby hid her relief that Bruce seemed to take for granted that he'd continue to be a part of her business. An employee. No, she decided, a partner, but she'd bring up the subject when they had a private moment. "I'll have to see about getting my own truck to replace my poor, tiny car that cries every time it has to travel that driveway."

Abby's father shook his head in puzzlement. "I never could understand why a building contractor as savvy as my dad practically ignored the driveway when he rebuilt the house. Why he didn't upgrade it so people could actually get here without destroying their cars in the process." He shook his head again. "It just doesn't make sense, never did but he wouldn't explain when I asked."

Grandma Maude chuckled. "Oh yes it does make sense, and that awful driveway was a deliberate decision." Conversation stopped at her words. "It was a nod to my childhood." They all looked at her in surprise. "When I grew up, this was wilderness. Real wilderness. You may think this is the wild north woods now but when I was young it was way wilder than it is today." She swept her hand to indicate the lake beyond the house. "Most lakes in the area now have houses all around them. They resemble suburbs more than wilderness."

"So?" Bruce's father couldn't follow her logic.

"The thing is, we owned half the lake and the other half was owned by a pioneer I grew up with who wanted it kept as pristine as we did and, since between us we owned all the lakeshore, we could do it. But there are always visitors who aren't necessarily considerate of the wilderness.

"So we got together and agreed to make it as difficult as possible to reach our homes. The result was a driveway that could be traversed but was so poorly constructed that only people determined to reach our places would make the effort. Take a chance on ruining their vehicle. Bump their way along until their bottoms were sore. Swear lots during the trip and wonder why we never improved any of it."

She looked straight at Bruce. "And when my neighbor sold his property, he made sure to sell it to someone who felt the same way." She nodded briefly but hard to emphasize her next words. "When you came along he checked you out before giving you a wonderful deal. We looked into your background and decided that you were the right person for this particular piece of forest when we learned that you grew up in the wilderness pretty much living the old way. So that's why you have it."

She looked from Bruce to Abby and back again, a satisfied expression growing as she regarded the two newest owners of the forest of her childhood. "You and Abby. The two perfect people to continue what is so loved about this lake and these trees."

Abby and Bruce stared at each other in shock as their parents' mouths dropped open and no one said a word because they were unable to speak. Until Bruce said, slowly and quietly, "So maybe the driveway should stay the way it is."

Abby nodded. "As a tribute to my grandfather – and my grandmother."

"And to remind us to never lose the wild feel of this special place."

Abby's mother began to laugh and kept it up until tears ran down her cheeks. "Wild? Really? Maybe the forest is wild, but not the house. It's a wonderful, extravagant reminder of a man who loved his wife enough to build her a house in the primitive wilderness she loved while loving his own comfort enough to make it the most up-to-date building imaginable."

Abby's father added to her words, thinking as he spoke. "It's the perfect place to both live and work and Bruce is right that trips to town to pick up supplies and make deliveries will keep this area untouched and pristine."

That evening, as things wound to a close and the older generations prepared for bed, Abby pulled on a parka and headed outside because she wanted to contemplate the driveway that she'd hated all her life.

To look at it through new eyes. To see it as an allay instead of the enemy. She stood for a long time looking down the corridor through the dark shadows of evergreen boughs meeting overhead along. And knew that it was perfect the way it was.

Her grandmother joined her, wrapped similarly in an oversized but extremely warm parka with sleeves that hung beyond her hands and a hood that almost concealed her face. "So now what?"

Abby smiled. "I talk to my friendly banker and ask about a loan to make this a place of work as well as a place to live."

"That's not what I meant."

Abby frowned. "If not the driveway or the kitchen, then what?"

"You, dear. Specifically, you and Bruce. You know, the man you're in love with who is in love with you, too, though neither of you seems in any hurry to do anything about it."

Abby's breath went out in a whoosh and she couldn't breathe for the longest time. Then she said, knowing it was futile to try and convince her grandmother that she wasn't in love with Bruce because Grandma Maude had always read her easily, "He doesn't know I exist beyond being a neighbor who constantly needs help and is a handy source of muffins."

"Which statement shows how blind you are." Grandma Maude sighed heavily. "But it's kind of a law of nature that the object of someone's affection is the last to know." She shook her head slowly, wagging it from side to side. "He's harder to read, though. I can't tell why he's not making his feelings clear." She pushed back the hood of her parka and shook her head in the crisp, cold air. "But he's not."

She regarded Abby closely. "Which means that if you hope for the happy future that I know is waiting for you when you two blind idiots start talking – really talking – to each other, then it's up to you to make the first move." She held Abby's gaze so Abby didn't dare look away. "So, tell me, dear. Are you going to do anything about this romance? Or not?"

Abby opened her mouth to answer. Stopped. Didn't know what to say. And simply burst into tears and ran into the house and her bedroom where she soaked her pillow and one white cat with tears before falling into a fitful sleep.

CHAPTER 21

She didn't stay asleep. Couldn't. Ended up in the main room of the house shortly before midnight, staring over the frozen lake and wondering what the future held. Whether her grandmother was right about Bruce's feelings for her. She was elderly, after all, and could have lost some of her uncanny ability to read people's emotions. She could be more hopeful than astute.

"I see you can't sleep either." Bruce's voice, inches behind her, made Abby jump. She was glad for the dark because she was afraid that in full light he'd read her thoughts and know what a fool she was.

His hand dropped onto her shoulder and pulled her back against him and she didn't resist. His heat warmed her and the electric buzz that always came with Bruce's touch moved through her body, bringing her fully alive and aching for more. "It's beautiful out there." Over her head, his gaze took in the now moonlit vista as she nodded because that was a safe thing, no voice that would crack was needed, and he could feel her nod against his chest.

They stood for a long time, no sound beyond their breathing, no lights beyond that of the moon and stars outside, no movement other than Bruce pulling Abby still closer until they were nestled together in spoon fashion with Bruce's arms around her. But it wasn't romantic, she told herself, merely friendship in the middle of the night.

"Seems to me that I once promised you a snowmobile ride."

She remembered. "Then your mother broke her leg and that was all that mattered."

"It's a beautiful night out. No wind, lots of stars and moonlight."

"Moonlight on the lake. Not beneath the trees." Which were black as ink.

"The snowmobile has headlights. I've never gotten lost yet and we've come and gone a number of times after dark."

She nodded the truth of that. "You know this area as well as my grandmother."

"I think I could navigate the driveway blind." A pause, then, "Which is why I'm suggesting that we take that snowmobile trek now."

"In the middle of the night?"

She felt his shrug. "Why not? I'm game if you are."

So they climbed into their warm outerwear as quietly as possible so as not to wake anyone, grabbed the keys to Bruce's snowmobile, tiptoed to the door that opened on silent hinges and chose the largest machine of the three in the yard, and then pushed it into the forest before starting it so as not to break the silence of the night any more than necessary.

And they went for their long-postponed ride. Along the driveway. Through the forest trail that branched from the driveway and led to Bruce's small home. Carefully, slowly, among the trees and through the strawberry patch where they first met. Then out onto the frozen lake where Bruce opened up until they fairly flew across the flat, white surface that in summer would be navigable only by boat. And all the time, Abby was behind him, arms tight around his middle, feeling that electric charge even through all the layers that kept them warm. And wished it was simple electricity but it wasn't. It was love.

Bruce stopped in the exact center of the lake and turned off the engine. The silence engulfed them, surrounding them with peace and something more. Something Abby couldn't describe but knew was what she'd come for, why she'd wanted the house in the forest, why she'd given up a job and a life in the city in exchange for the solitude and a totally different life in the wilderness.

A life that she wished she could share with Bruce.

And why not?

He wanted the same things out of life that she did. More than that, though, he was there when she needed him, offering advice and help even when she didn't ask for it, didn't want it, when she foolishly thought she could do without it. He was there for her, night and day, week after week, month after month.

Because he cared for her?

Could her grandmother be right?

Could he love her?

She wanted to know. Needed to know. Decided right then and there, in the moonlight, beneath the stars, in the center of the lake, on the night after Christmas, that she would find out.

The worst that could happen would be that he'd laugh at her and end their friendship and decide not to continue helping her make muffins.

No, he wouldn't laugh and he'd never end their friendship. He'd find a way to let her down as gently as possible and would continue to help whenever she needed it because that was the kind of man he was. And if her grandmother was right, he'd never be the first to speak of love so it was up to her.

So she took her heart in her hands, took a huge breath, and spoke into the vast silence of the night. "I want to say something."

"Okay." He turned halfway on the seat of the snowmobile to see her. Was silhouetted against the dim sky, a blocky bundle of parka and man but she couldn't see his face in the hood. "Is it important?" He tipped his head in thought. "Yes, it's important. Otherwise you'd not say anything." Because the silence was so beautiful. So awesome. So grand that they were lost in the winter world and the silence.

"Yes, it's important." She took another breath. "Very important." Another breath. "Very, very important. At least to me."

"Then shoot." But his voice cracked. He'd sensed something in her that told him what was coming was of extreme importance.

She cleared her voice a second time because she,

too, was finding it difficult to speak. "I just thought I'd mention that I'm in love with you." She shrugged as if it was no big deal. That he could laugh if he wanted and pretend she'd not said anything.

He didn't. Instead he drew in his own breath and held it so long she thought he'd die of suffocation. Let it out slowly and said, in a voice that was little more than a hoarse whisper, "Are you sure?"

She nodded. Wished she could see him in the dark, read his expression, see his eyes more than the shine that was dark eyes in the depths of his parka hood. "Yep. I'm sure." And cleared her throat again.

They sat there, staring at each other, unable to see what they were each thinking but knowing that the time had come for truth. For feelings.

Then Bruce spoke. "Good."

"Good? Is that all you have to say? Good?"

She saw it. Thought she saw it. A smile in that darkness that grew and grew until his whole face was filled with happiness. Or maybe she imagined it because the moonlight was no brighter and she couldn't see any better than moments earlier and she was simply imagining what she wanted to see.

No, it wasn't her imagination. It was the truth. Because he said, simply, "The feeling is mutual," on an outrush of breath as if he had to get it out as quickly as possible because he'd been holding it in too long.

They sat for another long moment. Then, slowly but with increasing speed, they moved towards each other. Bruce pushed Abby's hood aside and then his own. Then they kissed.

It wasn't the world's most wonderful kiss because they were encumbered by parkas and had to twist oddly on the snowmobile seat and couldn't truly see one another well enough to do it right. But they managed – somehow -- and later wondered how such a tame exchange between two people could send so much energy – and love – and electricity -- back and forth between them. And Abby knew at last that the fizz she'd felt for so long was mutual.

Bruce said something about the middle of the lake in the middle of winter not being the best place for discussions of a romantic kind and turned around on the seat and started the engine again, breaking the silence but this time it was a good thing, a wonderful thing because it meant they were heading full speed to the house in the forest where they could discard their bulky outerwear and actually see each other's faces as they discussed this new, amazing turn of events.

'Discuss' turned out to not be exactly the correct term, though some talk did happen in between other, more intimate, physical explorations. Like learning how lips tasted and felt. How a simple touch could cause shivers that seemed never to stop. Or the more fundamental experience of finding out that a love that was shared changed everything.

Then they got to the details. Like why Bruce had never said anything about his feelings for her. Why she'd had to make the first move. His answer was simple. "You come from way more money than I do. I never thought for a second that someone from a family like yours would even notice someone like me except when you needed help."

She snorted and laughed as she agreed that she'd needed help, remembering the times since they met that he'd saved her day. Or her business. Or her life. "It's true that I always seem to need help. Always will. And broad, strong, shoulders that can do things I can't. But make no mistake about it, mostly I need you. Just you." She emphasized her words by tapping him smartly on his shoulders and that led to a time during which neither said anything because they were too entwined to manage a word.

Until Bruce pulled back a bit and said, "How about we make this official?"

Abby's breath stopped. "I thought it was." But then she realized that she wanted to hear the words. The actual words. "What do you mean? Official how?"

He made a sound under his breath that said he knew exactly what she was thinking and she knew that knowing each other's thoughts – reading each other's minds – would be invaluable in the coming years. "I mean like what say we get married?" He pulled away a bit farther and thought over his words and knew they weren't right. Weren't the proper way to ask so he said it again, differently. Asked, "Will you marry me?"

Her answer was immediate. "Of course." Then, realizing that they were doing it exactly the way it was done in story-books, she changed it to, "Yes, I'll marry you."

After another long pause, he asked, "Should we wake everyone and tell them?"

They looked about the house. At the clock that was already heading towards morning of the day after Christmas. Abby shook her head. "It can wait."

He nodded agreement. "Then we'd best head to bed ourselves." And sighed mightily because they'd be heading for separate bedrooms. "What say we don't wait too long for that wedding?"

She considered his suggestion. And realized that the most important people to attend their wedding were already there. And that the house was decorated for Christmas and that would work for a wedding as well. "Good idea. Soon. Very soon."

She tipped her head back to try and see him but it wasn't easy in the dark as he repeated her thoughts. "No reason to wait. No reason at all."

And she caught the undertone of happiness that said he couldn't wait to become one with her as, with a sigh of what might have been regret – or happiness – he pulled completely away and headed for the stairs. "Morning can't come soon enough."

She peered out the window at the extra dark landscape because the moon had finally set and the northern lights had disappeared and the world was caught in the darkness that's the precursor of dawn. "Soon. Very soon, and we'd best get some sleep while we can because I suspect that once we tell everyone, we won't be able to sleep for a long, long time because they'll all be busy planning our future and, hopefully, including us in the planning."

CHAPTER 22

They both slept till noon. The rest of the household tiptoed around and asked each other how long Abby and Bruce had stayed up to be so tired. But, once the sleeping couple had risen, had lunch because breakfast was long gone, and managed to get everyone in one place at one time and told them that they were getting married, Abby's prediction came true.

"Wonderful." Grandma Maude couldn't be happier and managed not to say that now all the property around the lake would be in one family. At least, she didn't mention it until there was a pause in the conversation and then only in passing, though Abby knew her grandmother was overjoyed that the place she loved would continue as a complete and single piece of wilderness.

"When?" Abby's mother wanted to know the specifics. Pictures of dresses and bridesmaids and decorations floated through her head, everyone could see it. When Abby said 'soon,' her mother looked at the assembled people and the lovely, decorated house, and agreed that this time and this place was perfect as her vision of spring flowers was mentally replaced by poinsettias. "Let's get busy, people." She stood up and brushed imaginary crumbs from her designer jeans as she turned to Bruce's mother. "We have a wedding to plan."

Abby managed to find a small slice of private time to head to town with Bruce, where they spoke with the bank about a loan to turn the garage into a commercial kitchen and were given the go-ahead almost immediately. Then she stopped by Carolyn's to tell her they wouldn't be needing the building in town once their own kitchen was built.

She felt terrible about the news because Carolyn had enjoyed the monthly rent checks and could only hope that asking to purchase the equipment would make up for some of the disappointment. She was surprised when Carolyn danced across the floor because, without the expensive equipment that she'd had no other place to store sold to Abby and Bruce, the building would sell easily. In fact, there were a couple of people that she'd contact immediately.

That chore finished, Abby plunged into wedding preparations and was glad the wedding would be small and soon because, as she told Bruce during one of the few private moments since springing their news on everyone, she'd hate the planning that must go with a large wedding. His grunt said he understood completely.

So, not too much later, Bruce and Abby were married in front of the huge fireplace in the house in the forest, surrounded by family and friends who'd taken deep breaths and come north, left their cars and trucks by the highway, and let themselves be ferried to the wedding by snowmobile.

The pastor said it was one of the most unusual ways to get to a wedding that he'd ever experienced and commented that the wedding cake that the bride and groom had made themselves in the kitchen in town was the best he'd ever tasted and could he have the recipe, please?

They took a brief honeymoon in Bruce's one-room house because there were so many people in the house in the forest that privacy was impossible and they couldn't think of a single other place they'd rather be than in the wilderness.

Except the Caribbean because, once they were back in the forest house, Grandma Maude suggested they spend a week or so at her condo to 'make the honeymoon last longer' and get farther away than next door and mentioned that she was in no hurry to leave the place where she'd grown up. Not that she wanted to live there permanently, of course, but an extended stay would be enjoyable as she wanted to get to know Bruce's parents better.

They returned in three weeks with tans, ready to get to work. Because they had a business to run, a commercial kitchen to plan, a life to be lived, and furniture to move from Bruce's one-room home to the house in the forest where they'd spend the rest of their lives.

Together.

THE END

Dear Reader:

If you liked this book, I'll be forever grateful if you'll post a review on Amazon. Simply go to Amazon and type in _The Christmas House_ by Florence Witkop and then follow the prompts.

You also might like to read some of my other FGMN and TMA books so I've included a bit about each of them along with a link to find them on Amazon.

And here's a link to my website in case you want to learn more about my journey as a professional author, about my other books and short stories, or my thoughts on writing fiction. http://www.FlorenceWitkop.com

And happy reading to you all.

Florence Witkop

The first two books of the Johns Falls small town romance series can be found at:
Shh – Don't Tell
http://www.amazon.com/dp/B077RMTT2C

Recently jilted, Chloe Brown is back home in Johns Falls, Minnesota, working for her aunt selling furniture and other garden paraphernalia until she can recover emotionally, after which she'll leave.

When she discovers a family of Mallard ducks in one of the huge vases in the outdoor portion of the store, her aunt agrees to let them stay because protecting the ducks is taking her niece out of her severe depression.

Soon Chloe meets Ryan, short-term, interim manager of the Johns Falls newspaper. The two agree to support each other during this temporary, small-town stage of their lives, after which they will happily leave Johns Falls and each other. They find themselves sharing confidences, but Chloe has sworn to protect the duck family and keep them safe, so she keeps their existence a secret lest Ryan write about them in the paper, because a story could bring unwanted publicity, too many visitors, and possibly danger.

But secrets have a way of being uncovered, especially by experienced reporters.

And love isn't temporary.

A Very Black Cat

http://www.amazon.com/dp/B07BTGN58M

Welcome to Johns Falls, Minnesota, where everyone knows everything about everybody, often before they know it themselves.

So it's not surprising that two people who are falling in love are the last to know, even though everyone's talking about their romance and asking them personally for the lurid, juicy details. (Of which there aren't any because this is a clean, fun romance.)

But for the lovers to deny there's a romance even after being told straight out that they are in love? That's beyond belief. Meet Becky, dedicated small-town career girl following her pre-determined course to be the best bookkeeper in the area and now, with the blessings of her boss and all-around nice guy Tobias Whittaker, she'll also be a genuine business consultant with a framed diploma on the wall as soon as she finishes an online course that she'll fail without help from someone who understands the nuances of the people side of small town businesses.

Enter Jackson, hunky, former football jock and newish, charismatic owner of the lumberyard in town whose charm can convince the must obstinate customer to buy something,

whether that customer knew he wanted it or not, and whose boyish smile can subdue even the most stubborn heart but who can't keep his books straight no matter how hard he tries.
Add one small, black cat with a mind of its own into the mix that's not about to watch his two favorite people live without each other one second longer than necessary.

Then, along with the entire town of Johns Falls, Minnesota, sit back and enjoy the action.

The three books of the Legends Trilogy can be found at:
Spirit Legend
http://www.amazon.com/dp/B077TT5V53
Charlie, forester, guides her boss and the owner of Macallister Outdoors to a tiny lake in the middle of a wilderness tract he recently purchased so he can see with his own eyes the spirit that legend says lives there and uncover the truth about it. Suddenly, a rogue storm destroys the dam that created the lake, the surrounding forest, and much of their equipment. They are stranded.

Then they see the spirit and hear it sing. It's real, it's beautiful, and it will die when the lake drains dry. They resolve to patch the dam and save the lake and the spirit. As they work, they learn about the spirit of legend and about each other, while deliberately ignoring the growing attraction between them, because a romance between boss and employee is always a bad thing.

But some spirits can do more than just sing and look lovely.

And romance has a way of developing even when it's not wanted.
Wolf Legend
http://www.amazon.com/dp/B077WCSBB3
Jane, who dislikes wolves because they kill her livestock, takes

Buck Portman, wolf researcher and wildlife professor at a
nearby college she attends, to an island to seek out the huge
wolves of legend … the dire wolves of prehistoric times … that
local fishermen say they've seen there. She's skeptical until a
huge wolf runs through their camp and mentally connects with
Jane and invites her to visit so they can sort out this strange
mental phenomenon that neither of them expected.

Jane follows the wolf and Buck follows her into another world,
another dimension, one populated by larger-than-life dangerous
animals, including the wolves of legend. Her mental connection
to the alpha wolf is all that keeps them alive in this dangerous
world and when they return, at the request of the alpha female,
they take with them an injured wolf pup to be healed.

The pup heals nicely… but as it grows, will it remain a pet or
will it become a dangerous predator in a world where it doesn't
belong?

As the attraction between Jane and the professor grows, so do
the problems inherent in having a huge, prehistoric wolf in
today's world.

Earth Legend

http://www.amazon.com/dp/B077Y37FB8
Elle Olmstead isn't your normal, every-day botanist. She's
different. As a descendant of Ceres, goddess of the harvest and
fertility, she, like others of her family, has a magic touch with
plants. Real, honest-to-goodness magic. Which is why she
unwillingly stows away on the Destiny, a space ship filled with
ten thousand colonists heading for a distant planet. Because she
knows that her abilities are essential to keep the plants alive that
keep the colonists alive and that will be the basis for their
survival when they reach their destination.

She's caught and thrown in prison, where her powers are
useless. Soon the plants begin to shrivel and die. Starvation is
imminent, not to mention that the plants provide essential
oxygen. But no one believes her when she tells them who she is

and what she can do, especially not Cullen Vail, the one person she has come to like, maybe even love. Because Cullen is head of Security, an inscrutable, military type who has no time for stowaways and doesn't believe in foolish legends.

She lied before, why should he believe her now? But somehow she must persuade him of the truth or ten thousand people will die.

Made in United States
Orlando, FL
05 October 2022

23046007R00129